The Blue Diamond

Judith Whitworth

DEDICATION

In memory of my fourth son Frederikos, who loved my stories.

CONTENTS

PROLOGUE

"Will you please let Mr. Saint Austell Muir know that I am here?"

The young man behind the desk took the card offered and read it.

Karrendski. It was much easier handing out a calling card than trying to spell it. A pageboy appeared and led the upright old gentleman to the lift and when they arrived at suite number three, knocked. Algernon Karrendski handed the boy a coin, knocked again and went in.

"Hello, good morning, come on in. So here you are, Algie, bless you, bang on time of course." They shook hands warmly. "I've got champagne on ice, come on, let's crack it."

Algie's eyes opened wide.

"Already on the champers Roger? Isn't it normal to keep it for after the ceremony?"

A good pop rent the air and Roger carefully poured out two of the three glasses on the tray.

"Nothing is normal about us, old friend, which well you know," he raised his glass. "To our charming best man, and don't worry," grinning broadly, "there is plenty more for afterwards."

"And may I drink to you, highness. It hardly seems yesterday since I first met you, a charming, little boy. Good health and happiness Roger." So they both drank.

A door opened and a very attractive woman came in, her smile radiant. Both men went to her, faces full of admiration. She wore a deep blue silk

1

suit, very plain and beautifully tailored. Her hat consisted of the merest wisp of net of the same colour, which seemed to frame her face. Her hair, silver fair and freshly washed, glowed. A natural woman, she looked younger than her years. She kissed the newcomer, then held out her hand to the other, eyes glowing.

"You look wonderful, Maddy, my love."

"Well Madeline, I can't remember seeing you look so lovely." Both men speaking at once.

Madeline looked at them proudly. Roger, so tall, his white hair shining, just a little long, but it suited him that way, and everything about him gleaming from top to toe. Algie, older, slightly shorter and thinner, but so well dressed she could not fault him. She kissed him again, somewhat to his surprise and accepted her glass of champagne.

"We start early?" she quizzed Roger with a mischievous smile and sipped it approvingly.

A knock on the door alerted them and a pageboy came in carrying a florist's box. Madeline unwrapped it carefully, breathing in the sudden scent of flowers. There was a spray for her, blue and white, not large and very graceful and she felt tears well in her eyes. He thought of everything. There were also two small buttonholes for the men, so they busied themselves with pinning, standing back, admiring, finishing their champagne, while both men occasionally and surreptitiously glanced at their watches.

"And we have something else for you, Algie," said Madeline, opening her neat, deep blue, new bag. Taking out a small green leather box she handed it to him.

Puzzled, a smile on his face, he turned it over.

"Ah, my friends obviously have good taste, for they shop at Karrendski's." His voice a smile. Slowly he opened the box while the other two watched, their eyes bright in anticipation of his pleasure.

"Oh, oh my goodness!" Algie gazed in the box. "Oh but my dears, no, you should not have! The blue one?" Madeline leaned forward, took the box from him and carefully removed the tie pin set with the small, bright blue diamond.

"We decided that after all your help, Algie, this one was for you. Not only have you been a good friend to us, now, you are honouring us by being with us today." She leaned forward to set it into his tie. "May I? It won't spoil it?"

She carefully put the pin in his tie, and stood back.

Securely in place, Algernon Karrendski went to a mirror to admire his new and precious gift. Strangely, he had never been one for jewellery, but this was different.

"How can I thank you? Knowing what it is worth my dears, its rarity, your generosity is too much and my thanks quite inadequate."

"Don't thank us, Algie," Roger stood back and admired his friend, "thank my grandmother."

Then the phone rang and reaching for it, Roger spoke briefly. Turning to them smiling, taking Madeline's hand he said,

"The car is here, darling, Algie, shall we go?"

CHAPTER ONE

THE GIRL

"Drink!" Her eyes flew open to see a silver beaker directly in front of her face. She pursed her mouth tightly.

"Oh my jewel," her nurses' voice was low and beseeching. "Hark! She is coming now, I beg you to drink, or she will be very angry."

Sushila half turned her head so that the girl who was brushing her hair had to stop. Yes, sure enough, she could hear the approaching sound of her aunt, her loud voice, her clanging, jangling bracelets. As a widow, technically her aunt should not be wearing jewellery. But, the girl sighed, it had its uses, they always knew when she approached. She looked past the beaker at the anxious eyes of her ayah, the most beloved person in her life.

With a quick gesture, her ayah lifted the cup and drank, as if to prove it was palatable, then she pushed it at her stubborn charge. As the curtain swept aside, her aunt came in, a look of satisfaction on her face. Sushila drank what was left, pulled a face and then gazed at her aunt with disdain.

"What poison is it you give me now, aunt? Do you want me dead? Don't think I do not know what you are doing. Just because I am young, you think I am stupid, and I am not."

"Brush her hair, girl," her aunt shouted and the brushing resumed with force. "Do I pay you to stand with your mouth open and the hairbrush in the air?"

Sushila narrowed her eyes. "You do not pay her," she thought, "my father does." But she held her head steady to let the poor little maid make up for the few precious moments lost.

"How can you say such things," her aunt fussed about the room, probably as usual looking for something to complain about. "Every bride has nerves, and every bride has great demands put upon her at this most important day of her life. All you have had to drink is a calming tea, nothing more. Now!" She turned to leave the room, changed her mind, "Ayah, make sure she bathes properly, then call me and we will come to dress her."

She turned to stand directly in front of the girl. "And you, niece, remember you are, despite everything, about to become a rani, behave like one. Conform to the right ways, do not always be so stubborn, so," she hesitated, "different!"

She fingered the glorious silk sari which lay on the bed, admiring the glow of red and gold which shone from every fibre. More quietly she repeated, "When you are bathed we will come to dress you and then you must come to my room for the jewels."

"Ayah can dress me as usual, aunt, and she always bathes me perfectly!"

Sushila again twisted her head to look at her aunt. "And I do not want to be laden down with jewels like a nautch girl for sale. I am not, I repeat, NOT, getting married. I want to learn, to go to school, maybe to be a doctor!" Her aunt let out a shocked gasp before turning on her heels and walked out. Then more quietly, Sushila almost sobbed, "I do not want to get married, until I want to. I do not want to marry that boy!" Her cry was almost a wail.

Oh what an awful woman. Sushila gazed through half closed eyes at her father's retreating eldest sister with loathing. She had been actually smiling, the old toad, a sort of resigned, silly smile. "I hate you," she muttered under her breath. "You have arranged this marriage because you want me out of the house, so that you can take over." What use to fight and struggle against the inevitable. They had arranged everything. She was as the smallest piece on her father's chess board. She had no say in anything, even her own life.

A tear slipped from an eye and her nurse rushed forward, the corner of her soft white cotton sari gently pressing against her cheek to soak it up.

"Cry not, my little dove," she said, "do not spoil your beauty." Gently, she drew her close, took the hair brush from the girl and began the familiar, soft strokes.

"Be kind, my pet," the gentle voice admonished her, "for remember, your aunt, the poor thing was a child bride, and a child widow. What joy has she ever had in her life? Be kind, my dove, just think, tomorrow you will be a married woman, you can feel kindly for your poor old aunt who had nothing in her life."

"But ayah darling," Sushila gave an involuntary sob, "I truly do not want to get married, yet."

"I know, my jewel, I know."

"He is not such a special boy, you know that too, don't you, ayah?"

"Hush, my child, let no one hear you, or that you have seen him or I will be cast aside and then you will be alone."

It was so comfortable and safe, leaning against the soft cotton of her beloved nurses' sari. And she was right. At all costs she must be kept near, for without her, life would be too frightening. Even so, knowing the bad luck she was labelled with, her mother having died at her birth, Sushila knew it must have been hard for her father to find her a fine bridegroom. And certainly, despite the fact she was not ugly, indeed darling ayah always said she was beautiful, the dowry he was paying was enormous. She recalled the one glimpse she had of her future husband.

They had crept, ayah and she to a small balcony and looked down into the garden where the men were sitting. Torches flamed, set into the earth all about the terrace where her father, uncles and brothers were with the groom and his men folk. The smell of cheroot smoke and gurgle of their hookahs rose while they spoke, although their words were unintelligible, intermingled with the clack of worry beads.

"He is handsome, is he not, my love?" Ayah whispered.

She paused for a moment, trying to see the stranger in the dim light of the flares. Perhaps he was handsome, but he was too fat and he had a double chin. Of course she said so.

"Better a plump husband, than one all bones, my love. A slightly lazy man is easier to handle that a thin, active one."

Sushila had rested her hand on her nurses' cheek and smiled.

"You are so wise, ayah darling," she whispered, "and I love you. Thank you for this, now let us go quickly before we are seen."

So at least she knew what he looked like, and everyone assured her of his good nature. Perhaps she would be lucky after all, despite the signs of her birth. Even so, she was still only thirteen and she did not wish to get married, yet.

Ayah took her hand and pressed something into it.

"It is of no value my lady, none at all, but it is pretty, and I have nothing else to give you. Keep it for good luck as I have. For it was given to me by your mother, just before she died when I first came, she told me in her soft voice, that as a child she had found it in a stream bed, a pretty blue stone as a chick pea, that it was of no worth, probably glass, and so gave it to me, a thanks gift, and see, we have been so happy." She pressed the little head against her breast again for a moment and again pushed the small, cold thing into Sushila's hand.

Looking at it, the girl saw an intense blue stone, like a large pea, a pebble, set in a simple silver setting.

"I will have it re-set my dearest ayah, and I will treasure it always, for first it was my own mothers, then, it was yours, the mother of my life. I thank you," and gently kissed her.

CHAPTER TWO

THE WOMAN

"Drink!" The voice was gentle, somehow an echo. "Drink, my dove, for you must be so tired and your poor little body needs sustenance."

Sushila held the hand with the cup trying not to tremble and drank. Indeed, she was thirsty. It was milky, with the taste of honey and almonds, cool and comfortable. She closed her eyes.

"Is he alright, ayah?" she asked in a small voice. The furious cries of a new-born could be heard from the next room.

"Ah, my clever love, he is a fine prince. You have been so brave! His Highness is greatly pleased and has already been to see his son." Very gently, her hand swept back the damp hair on the girl's forehead. "What a clever one you are, an heir, I do not doubt that His Highness will be calling the jewellers so that he can choose some great reward for you, who have done so well."

Sushila lay in semi-oblivion. She had not wanted to marry and they had made her, but at least she had done her duty, produced a son, done the correct thing. She had never imagined that childbirth could be so terrible and knew in her heart, that she could never go through it again. Never!

She lay, a small, very young woman, only half aware of what was going on about her. The raucous cries of the crows filtered through the small every day domestic sounds, and now her little son was quiet, she turned her head into the softness of her pillow and slept again.

For many days after the birth, all the women of both families came with tender smiles and sumptuous gifts for the poor, exhausted little mother. There were so many of them. They came on tiptoe, smiling proudly, with their children, their mothers-in-law, their sisters-in-law, their ayahs, all clustering around. Their gentle smiles and praise did indeed make Sushila happy, as indeed did the little prince who suckled furiously from his wet nurse.

"You are too young to nurse your child," had announced her aunt, directing her ayah to pull tight the bands which held her aching breasts. And oh, she was so thirsty and they would only give her tiny sips of water.

"It will pass," said a sweet cousin. "You are so young, you do not want to spoil your shape. Let the wet nurse care for him, so you can be free."

It did pass, and soon she was playing mah-jong, chess and checkers with her visitors who continued their visits, cooing over the baby prince, building up her confidence, and showing off their own handsome children. It was a joyful palace, with much coming and going. Guests staying, or guests just visiting. Many of the important men of the district, came to congratulate the young raja which pleased him greatly. It was a supremely happy place.

Then one evening, a little boy, his eyes overly bright, held his nurses' hand and said,

"My throat hurts, ayah." So was quickly whisked away to his own home.

Three weeks later, there were many more sore throats, many little children with swollen necks, and a few really ill adults, including His Highness.

The foreign doctor stood before the young rani, absently swinging his stethoscope. He had come to this small principality chiefly to find good country girls to take back to the city to train as nurses. Yet he had returned, liking the coolness and the green, rolling hills and set up a small practice and enjoyed his relatively quiet life. His eyes down on her feet, for it didn't do to look into the eyes of these high born Indian ladies, the gold rings on her toes fascinated him, he supposed one got accustomed to wearing them, as with on the fingers.

"Rani," he said, surprisingly in her own language but with a terrible accent. "Your husband is grievously ill. Send your baby to the hills, do not have him return until this sickness is past." He paused for a moment, staring at the beautiful still figure of the small woman before him. "Woman!" he thought. "Nowt but a slip of a girl, fancy putting her with child before even she is full grown." He coughed, uneasy. Almost as an aside, very softly so she just caught it, he said,

"Keep the little prince very safe, for I doubt that your husband will sire any more children."

Which is how it was. At first he had blamed her, that proud young raja, when month after month, year after year, no second child was born. Then he had brought many girls to the palace, strutting about as a peacock, blaming everyone of them but himself, for apparently, no more children were conceived.

Sushila closed her doors against the constant and loud music which came from her husband's quarters. What an embarrassment, flaunting those women in their home, she felt her face grow cold with the shame of it. So she spent her days playing with her little son and remembered the quiet words of the foreign doctor. Few friends came to visit at this time, so he had for awhile no playmates.

Then, eventually, her husband went to the city for some days, and came back surprisingly quiet. Understanding that he had been to see doctors, the young rani did what she could to dismiss the tragedy to his manhood by showing him his sturdy little son as often as possible. Undoubtedly, the raja was greatly proud of his heir, but of further children, there were no more. That childhood illness had seen to that.

CHAPTER THREE

CONTENTMENT

The seasons passed and the little prince grew strong and tall. It was a problem not allowing everyone to spoil him, and Sushila and ayah were very firm with his nurses, which was not easy. A way around this was to invite many friends and family once more to stay with their children. In this way he had play mates and the palace was a noisy, joyful place again, often it seemed, overfull with children.

Regularly, Sushila called musicians to come and each child received a small instrument to play along with them, which was a huge success.

Dancers came too, but country woman, not the fanciful city dancers who always were so suggestive in their movements. The little girls had dancing lessons, and Sushila's friends were grateful to her as music and dancing were most acceptable in their society, and would in time, add to their children's attributes. Although so young, marriage was always at the back of the mother's minds, and being at the palace was alone a great privilege.

Then sometimes, the gully-gully man would come to the huge delight of the over excited children. Spell bound they would watch his tricks, things appearing and disappearing under little copper pots, and the ayahs had quite some difficulty in controlling them.

When the poor wife of the gully-gully man was put into a basket and sent to perhaps Bangalore, or Delhi, they watched spellbound as the sword was pushed, this way and that, into the basket, so surely the woman was not there. But when he called her to come back, they heard her thin voice reply, so finally she came slowly out of the basket, rocking and heaving and everybody clapped. Sushila always gave ayah a good coin to secretly give the poor woman for it cannot have been a very comfortable task or good life. At least, when they had finished their show and been paid, they were led to the kitchens for a meal. If she could have stopped the gully-gully man from so using his wife, Sushila would have, but it was traditional and everybody expected it.

Other times, traders would come and spread their wonderful wares all over the cleanly swept verandas. Now this was the time for the ladies and the children were banished. It took hours, more and more lovely saris and shawls, blouse pieces and cloth for the children's clothes, came out of the huge bundles, it was so difficult to choose. Finally came the bargaining, which took just as long, bitter complaints from both sides, yet it seemed in the end, everybody was happy.

After these great purchasing events, the tailors came, men, sitting on a cushion on the floor, drawing with chalk, cutting, with their mouths filled with pins, and finally bringing out their treasured sewing machines. The trying on of the half made clothes was tiresome and a few slaps were heard on difficult children.

"Will you run naked like the street children then?" admonished exasperated mothers.

Before long the fine new clothes were made and accepted and there was peace, till the next time.

All the traders, tailors, musicians and gully-gull men who came, were very proud of their connection with the palace, especially as there were so many families there, and business was good.

For feast days, just the ladies were invited into Sushila's suite. With the doors closed, the punka walla bribed to work hard to give them some breeze, the jewellers brought out their glorious pieces, for it was the correct thing to do, to celebrate the feast day. It was Sushila who always bought the finest pieces, delighting in their colour, workmanship and she would show her son,

"These are for your bride, my prince, for without daughters, I must have someone to give them to." So the prince would play with the jewels, put them on and laugh.

The jewellers were also very patient for the rani always asked questions about the gems. One young jeweller, a son, had studied gems indeed and delighted in answering his rani's questions, bringing rare or uncut stones to show her. Whenever he had something special, he would send a message and be summoned. Then she would pour over the treasure, and probably buy it.

Under her sari, hidden away amongst her other jewels was the simple little gold basket in which nestled the blue stone which ayah had given her and which her own mother had found in a stream bed when a child. This was her greatest treasure, a special gift.

As the prince grew older he was taught to ride, first a small, elderly pony, and eventually a horse almost as fine as his father's. Two grooms always rode with the prince, and the boy loved his dawn rides, and came after his bath to greet his mother for the day, always with something new to tell her.

Sushila felt a great pride in her son, for according to his teachers, he was diligent, if not particularly clever, something which his mother insisted on knowing, and certainly he was amiable. The fact that despite being an only child and a prince, he was not too spoiled, was a boon. He was kind, friendly and biddable, therefore everyone liked him and Sushila thanked the gods for that.

When the prince turned 13, the rajah summoned his wife and son to his quarters, there to meet a very tall European man.

"Rani," he bowed, "I am headmaster of Saint Mathew's College and his highness tells me he wishes his son to become a pupil."

Sushila felt faint for a moment then turned on her husband, gave him a very hard look, and walked out. A battle began, this time, for once, the prince siding with his father and leaving Sushila furious. While she stayed in her rooms weeping and raging, apparently their highnesses simply got on with their preparations and smart new European clothes were made, a smart college uniform, which greatly pleased the young boy.

"And I will learn good English and French, and cricket and hockey and Rugby. Mother dearest, I am so excited."

Sushila watched her son and realized that perhaps for the first time, she had lost a battle but realized that her son was truly happy.

"And, my dove," said ayah, "he will meet other young men, from good and intelligent families, surely that is a good thing?" All the while gently brushing the luxurious black and shining hair. So Sushila accepted that her only child was growing up, and to the surprise of everyone, and huge gratitude of the headmaster, and indeed the parents, the boys and as well as the town, she handed him the deeds of twenty acres of land, for playing fields, being part of her dowry.

If she had made no decision for her son to attend the college, she could be magnanimous, and surprise them all.

CHAPTER FOUR

LIFE

"But I do not wish to marry, yet, mother," another echo. Sushila looked up at her son, it was a constant surprise to her how tall he was at eighteen.

"I know, my dear child. But I beg you to, for my sake, for all our sakes. You are the last one. Once you have a child or two, then you can travel as you wish, visit foreign countries, this I promise. But first, I beg, I implore you to marry."

"How can I do this to him?" she thought, "I, who have been through it myself. But I had brothers and sisters, he has none."

"Look for yourself, my son. I will let you choose your own bride. Any caste, any family. Things are changing nowadays, you will have my blessing if she is a strong, good girl. You need not ask for a dowry, we need nothing. A healthy girl from a decent, devout family, that is all I ask."

To her surprise, he did as she asked. Well, however privileged he had been, he had always been kindly and biddable. What was more, he surprised them for he chose well. Of course the girl's family had little money, for as the rani discovered during her enquiries, the grandfather had speculated unwisely. The girl was a fraction taller and older than he, very fair skinned with grey eyes and a sweet disposition. Not a particularly beautiful girl, but, pleasant enough to look on.

It was a grand wedding. When the astrologer gave the date, the bride's family seemed somewhat surprised by the speed of things. Even so, they came in their droves, overwhelming her, for most were tall too, she noted, real Northern people.

She liked her daughter-in-law. It was good having a young friend in the palace, someone to show around, to teach, to sing with. Out came the jewels and Sushila rejoiced in teaching her son's wife the names and attributes of the beautiful stones. When she had forgotten some fact, the knowledgeable jeweller was summoned to entertain the two enthusiastic ranis.

Not only was the bride gentle and kind, she was always smiling. Almost immediately she became pregnant, which Sushila considered was another reason to feel that her son had made a most satisfactory choice. When, within the year, a son was born, fair with grey eyes as his mother, Sushila told her son, "Now you can go. Travel, see the world, come back after a year and have another child and meanwhile I will care for this one."

Joyfully they set off on their travels, every bit the maharaja and maharani of their domain. Letters came from distant lands, they sent photographs, gifts, mementos which could not be carried with them. A grand tour it was, which did not last so long, for as the bride was again expecting a child, they came home. In no time, a tiny girl was born, and the palace nurseries were alive with life once more.

The rani's ayah prayed fervently to the gods, taking gifts, the sweetest flowers and most expensive incense to the puja room. So much for the bad luck, which had been labelled on to her beloved mistress. See, see, all was well with her and her family. Stiffly she rose, her knees cracking and she brushed away the small shadow of doubt which passed over her mind. How could bad luck stick to an innocent child? No, all was well and she held her head high as she silently walked barefooted on the cool marble floors to her mistress's apartment.

How fortunate she had been, a simple, little maid servant, to have caught the baby girl who had been born so early. How wonderful it had been for her to have something of her own to love, and the baby had known this, and loved her in return. She was her life now, and she would protect her till her dieing days, the gods had heard and been kind.

15

CHAPTER FIVE

TAMASHA

Everything was prepared and ready. The elaborate pavilions and great tents were cleverly placed about the grounds. They were sumptuous and every one had fine carpets laid on the ground for the guests to sit on. Near to the verandas, the long, white clothed tables and chairs stood neatly ready for the Europeans. Servants hovered, eagle eyed, guarding the shining silver and gold plate which lay thickly everywhere. Musicians played softly in the distance, so altogether, it was a magnificent event.

Sushila looked at herself in the long glass. Not so much changed, she thought. A little plumper, certainly, but that was natural for a woman of her age. Her ayah brushed her beautiful, long, dark hair with firm sweeps, something she must have done thousands upon thousands of times. Carefully, Sushila looked at her beloved nurse. Had she grown smaller? Was she really so grey?

"Ayah, dearest, why don't you put walnut juice on your hair, to keep it dark? Why do you take so much trouble with my hair and nothing for your own?"

A slow smile crossed the familiar face, yet she kept on brushing.

"Ah, my queen, you were always such a foolish little monkey. Your old ayah is a servant, of low caste, a nothing. Why should I labour to keep beautiful?"

They were silent for awhile, the hair brushing matching the soft swish of the punka.

"I was but a little maid servant when you were born, ten years old was I, carrying towels into your lady mother's room. You know the story well. It was chance which put me there to receive you into my hands when the lady gave birth so suddenly, for just then, unusually, no one else was in the room. From that moment I loved you, from that moment I was your slave. It was my good fortune that when, poor soul, she died, it was I alone who seemed able to quieten your lonely cries. Even the wet nurse could not. So here we are my angel, still together. And I am so proud of you, for you are at the age when women are most beautiful. The foreigners will gaze at you with envy, for you are far more lovely than their own women."

Sushila looked at herself critically in the mirror. She supposed time had been kind to her. Because of the illness which had swept the palace shortly after her son's birth, she was not worn out by bearing her husband more sons. At least her son was a fine young man and his wife had already borne him two enchanting children.

"We have been blessed, ayah. Unlike my mother, I am not worn out with child bearing, and, thanks to the gods, our house is secure with healthy children."

The brushing stopped midway down the sweep of gleaming, black hair.

"Hush, my child, for it is bad luck to speak so," and made a gesture with her hand to ward off the evil eye. "Now come, you know how these foreigners always arrive so promptly and stand about waiting to be served."

Deftly, she plaited the thick hair, twisted jewels and jasmine into the tail and stood back to admire her work.

"You are more beautiful than ever, my little dove, come now, His Highness will surely need urging along."

It was a great and successful durbar. Many important people had come, Indians and Europeans of the highest rank. What was more, it had been remarkably well organized, and Sushila realized that her husband's new secretary, the Portuguese-Indian, Mendoza, had been the cause of it. A tall, pale young man, very quietly spoken, he nonetheless persuaded one and all to do his bidding. With sheets of closely written paper in his hands, he seemed to be everywhere at once. It amused her to note that the generally shouting and arguing staff were obliged to be silent in order to hear his quiet orders. On a previous and smaller occasion, many had suddenly found themselves without a job and home, because Mendoza decreed they had not done their tasks well enough. So clever.

The mahouts had handed up their passengers into the splendid howdahs on top of their beloved elephants. Of course they had had to borrow some, as there were too many people for their own stable. Mendoza had organized that too, by skilfully inviting the right rajas. Every room in the palace was filled with guests, while some had brought their own luxurious tents which were placed about the gardens.

Meanwhile the women stayed in the background, a blaze of coloured silk and jewels, their children running wild with ayahs running behind them. This was a quarter where Mendoza had no influence.

Sometimes the European ladies came to meet the rani, usually great big, pink women. A few of them could converse with her, and Sushila was intrigued. Tiny, she was dwarfed by them, yet she was pleased to observe all she could of their clothing, their skin and hair colour and of course, it was obvious that they were observing her too. Some stayed for a few days, while the Indian guests settled in happily to stay for as long as they could.

Just when they were congratulating themselves on the great success of their house party, an illness swept through the remaining guests. A visitor's maid-servant became ill first, then the children who she minded, followed by palace servants. Eventually the palace was emptied while families fled to their own homes, taking the sickness with them. An old local doctor came and hopefully made up herbal teas.

The fever ran high, and the parents wrung their hands with anxiety. Wise women came with more herbs, and the whole palace seemed tense and quiet except for the cries of the sick. It was all too often so, when a big group of people met together.

"It cannot be," the rani's ayah muttered to herself as again she knelt in the puja room. "I have prayed, I have made offerings! Why is this happening to us?"

CHAPTER SIX

ACCURSED

"Polio, sir," had said the young English doctor with the governor's party. "I'm afraid it will mostly affect the children. I am trying to instruct them not to panic and to isolate, but it is difficult. That Portuguese secretary, Mendoza, is a huge help, for not only does he know the language, he knows their ways. I regret to say that there is very little we can do."

"Do we have any treatment for this dreadful illness?" asked his superior.

"Sadly sir, I fear not, there is little which really works. Theirs is more faith healing, than anything else. They grind up pearls and precious stones to mix with their medicines in the firm belief they will help. Perhaps psychologically it does."

A soft snort came from one of the young officers.

"No chance they will be any use to anyone, I can assure you," said young Karensdski. "A sort of witch craft, using the lowest quality of gem, yet, poor souls truly believe in it."

"Do what you can, Doctor Muir. I'm afraid the rest of us must leave but I think it would be politic if you stay, if you are willing of course."

Doctor Muir did stay, his two servants erected his tent in the shade of a fine tree close to the palace and he settled in.

Filipe Mendoza wisely introduced the young foreign doctor to the local one. The thin, little Indian peered up at the tall, fair foreigner and smiled. Despite their outward differences, they seemed to have an immediate empathy while barely having any language in common. Their eyes expressed a great deal, but, somehow, having met, they both felt that they had an ally.

So many little children became ill, Sushila was frantic and begged Mendoza to ask the foreign doctor for advice. To her surprise, he came, helping the old doctor attending all the sick. Then he announced that he would stay on, until the illness had abated, long after the governor's party had left, on call, living in his tent in the grounds, should he be needed.

"Why is he doing this?" the rani asked the secretary.

"Because he is a doctor, highness, as well as being a good man."

The days passed in a hot, humid, nightmare of sorrow. Whispers and incense from the prayers to the gods, wafted throughout the high rooms. Prayers, bells and gongs were a daily sound as the priests took the dead away, quickly on silent, bare feet.

Then the young raja and his rani died with their little daughter, quick and painful deaths. The little son became ill, so grievously ill that a terrified Sushila and her ayah took him into her rooms to tend him.

The foreign doctor came, went over the child, bathed him in cool water, and showed the women what to do. At night he ordered them to sleep, while he sat beside the child, holding the hot little hand.

Then, very suddenly, the old raja died in the night, and the rani pressed her forehead onto his feet, unbelieving. Despite the fear of contagion, many came to attend his funeral and to bear him away to the burning ghats. Horns blew, gongs rang, the smell of flowers barely covered the sickly stink of death in the day's fierce heat.

"Doctor Muir," the secretary bent close. "Sir, I need your assistance. The raja is being taken away, and there is talk of suttee." The foreigner's eyes opened wide. The secretary nodded.

"Believe me, sir, if she is found alone, some of the elders might secretly take her. I beg you to keep close, for despite the British laws, some of these people are religious fanatics and occasionally do manage to drug the widows, then take them away to burn with their husbands."

A new order was hastily arranged. Sushila's room was turned into a ward, with the little boy and three others in a row of cots, while the rani and her ayah cared for them. The door was locked to everyone except the doctors. Only the ayah went out, for food and water, but usually to cajole the punka boy to pull his rope harder to make some cool air for the sick. Talk of installing electricity had gone on for years yet had come to nothing. At least the punka wallah stayed at his post and did not run away as had many others.

When at last the four patients were obviously on the mend, Sushila felt the fever overcome her.

"I am only tired," she told her ayah. "Be sure, all I need is sleep." Yet she was wrong. The days and nights which followed were as a very bad dream. Terrible heat, choking, fighting for breath, icy cold, and always strong arms, a soft hand and a gentle voice.

When the fever abated, the rani, drawn and thin had gazed at her nurse in horror.

"You mean you left me?" The rani, well again but terribly weak, found energy to be ferociously royal. "You left me alone with a foreign man?" Her loving nurse just managed a small smile, grateful to see that her beloved child was well again. But oh, the fatigue, the sheer bliss to sleep.

He had taken her to the room next door where two mothers were now tending the healing little patients. He asked for water, cloths, a hand fan, and she had given them to him, wholly trusting.

"Did he bathe me?" the querulous voice went on. "I thought it was you, of course. How could you let a man, a strange, foreign man, touch me. Indeed he must have seen all my body." The voice became tearful.

"He is a doctor my angel. He knew what to do, and he saved you. I was too tired for anything, he saw that and there was no one else, they have all gone away. Be not ashamed my dove, yours is a beautiful body, if indeed he saw it. For he treated you exactly as he had all the others, only to try to take down the fever."

The tired little rani closed her eyes and thought about it. When a cool hand took hers, pressed fingers on her wrist, she did not stir. When the fingers were removed, her hand was still held, very tenderly. Greatly daring, she lifted it up and held it before her eyes.

The skin was about the same colour as hers, yet the hairs on the back of the hand were golden, but then, so was his hair. She wondered how old he was, this courageous young foreigner who had stayed to nurse them. Probably a little younger than she was. When she looked up, she saw the blue eyes, a deep blue, not like the wishy-washy mixed race colours from centuries of invaders, so many of their family had. Greeks, Persians, who knew who else. He was smiling at her. Then she pressed the back of the hand to her mouth and held it there for a moment.

"I am greatly indebted to you," she said weakly, and he merely nodded, not understanding her words, yet still, understanding. So she drifted back into sleep, a small smile on her face.

As she got better, her small grandson would be laid beside her and she would tell him stories, sing and play little games with him. When the doctor came, he always had some little treat for the child before he began to exercise his legs. For they now realized that all was not well and that they did not work properly, one leg particularly. The child complained loudly, while the doctor sang, some foreign child's song, so the secretary said. He was firm, yet kind, always trying to get the child to teach him Hindi as a distraction, while the leg was moved, backwards and forwards.

"One two, buckle my shoe, three four, knock on the door, five six," and so forth. Mendoza translated for them, using the Hindi words, so the distraction did work to a point.

Ayah squatted quietly in the background observing as she always did. She did not like the half-caste, Mendoza, poor pale, skinny thing that he was. Yet she realized the rani's need for such a man, as well as recognising the same streak of faithfulness in him which she had. So she took to doing small kindnesses for him, and always seeing that a glass of cold lime juice was set beside him whether or not the doctor was present too. Of course Mendoza thought that this was by order from the rani.

Let him think what he liked, it was imperative that he kept well for all their sakes.

The day came when the doctor had to leave.

"Get in touch with me if there is need," Doctor Muir requested of the secretary.

"Certainly doctor, but have no fear now, she is safe."

They all saw him off with garlands and tears. Sushila accepted the foreign way of shaking hands, yet again lifted it to her mouth and pressed her lips to it in gratitude. All she felt was a surprisingly heavy weight in her heart as she stood on the veranda waving, her small grandson beside her. They were well again certainly, except for the boy's leg which they would faithfully exercise. So why did she feel so ill still?

"Life will get back to normal again soon," her ayah said quietly. "Truly this has been a bad time for us. But we were lucky, at least there are two left. Now you must get strong for the little raja, my dove. It is your task now, to keep him safe and well."

CHAPTER SEVEN

SORROW

A paler, thinner Sushila tried to fill her empty days with reorganizing the palace. It seemed a desolate, echoing place now that her husband, son and family had died. Indeed, everyone had left. Gone were the regular, busy sounds of the day, calls of nurses, the squeals of children, general coming and going. The heat was oppressive, the dust trodden or blown in with the faintest of breezes. Even the crows were silent except early and late in the day. All was quiet except for the chipkillies ticking away on the ceilings.

As there were fewer people to attend to, there were fewer servants and those who remained were recovering themselves or mourning their own losses. So it was that Sushila's poor ayah was running all day, exhausted herself, much thinner, but determined that life should go on, and that standards would be kept up. There were no excursions or guests to prepare for, no longer did the halls bustle with people waiting for audience or friends waiting to see the royal family. So she had decided weakly, that this was the moment to urge her mistress into cleaning out, sorting, room by room, throwing away years of clutter, repairing, white washing.

"It could," the secretary told the rani after he had informed her that despite the tragedy, the coffers were comfortably full, "it could be the moment to install electricity, just as His Highness always planned? We can then white wash when it is done." For the first time in weeks, Sushila felt a surge of optimism and gave Mendoza the order to go ahead. A therapy.

The minimum of the household moved to the rani's old home only visiting the palace once a week to inspect the progress.

The installation of electricity inevitably was a noisy and dusty affair, three months of mess and inconvenience. A miracle it might be to have electric lights and fans, but when it was done and order restored, the palace freshly painted, gleaming white, the little rani again fell into a decline, sitting on her veranda in the shade, staring out at the fountains in the garden, dull, sad. There was so little to do now, no one to speak with, or sing with. Except her little grandson who was at least now running about the grounds, limping a little but still running. She had no plans for anything ahead, just time stretched, and she felt so alone. Surely she was accursed.

"Highness," the secretary bent over her chair, speaking quietly. "It might be clever to hold an audience, to let the people see that you are well again and that you are able to run the kingdom without your husband." She listened, but the emptiness in her heart weighed her down so heavily, the last thing she could do was to make decisions.

"Highness," the quiet voice persisted. "Think of something. Something to lift the spirits of the bereaved, something to give hope." For you too, highness, he thought.

It had slowly come to Sushila why she was so despondent. At first she had thought she was merely weak and exhausted and that in time she would heal. Then she thought perhaps that she was missing her husband, that foolish man, her son, daughter-in-law and the baby girl. Trying to see their faces in her memory, she found she could hardly remember them and, unusually for her, she wept. She realized only that it would have totally crushed her soul if the little boy had also died. For his life, she thanked the gods daily, faithfully worshipping, grateful for what was left.

Gradually, during her long, waking, miserable hours, it came to her, the truth of her malady. She was shocked, appalled with herself, yet it could not be denied. She missed the foreign doctor and thought of him every waking hour and when she did sleep, she dreamed of him. Imagine, she thought wryly, she a rani, a queen of her people, important and wealthy, was as a village girl, yearning for an unobtainable love. Where up till the great sickness, she had been totally mild in all things, now her temper had grown short. Now anyone who irritated her in the smallest degree had a lashing from her tongue. What had happened to her? Accursed, accursed!

Then it came to her in a beautiful dream, the solution. He was standing there by her bed, as he had so often during her illness, his blue eyes alight with a smile.

Her hand on her heart she asked, "What can I do to ease this pain, doctor Sahib?" And clear as clear he had replied.

"You could make a hospital for the town," he said, in Hindi too. "If there is another epidemic, it would be a great service to your people."

Sushila rose, her heart light. It was a miracle, her dream, an omen. Now she knew what to do, he had told her, she would start immediately. Her ayah looked up from her pallet from under her draped sari and saw the change.

"Sit, Mendoza, sit!" She waved her hand at him crossly, her golden bracelets chinking prettily, for even if she had criticised her widow aunt all those years ago, she loved her jewels and disregarded the unwritten law that widows should be unadorned. "My neck hurts when I have to look up at you, sit, please."

Filipe Mendoza sat on the edge of his chair with a pad on his knee ready to jot down her orders.

"I want you to write a letter to the governor, asking him to send Doctor Muir to me. It is my intention to build a hospital for all our people here, and I need his help. Now," the hands waved again tinkling. "A short and polite letter, and one which shows I will not take any excuses for him not to come. The governor will understand that this is a great gift for the people. We may be a small kingdom, but we shall be modern," she waved a bejewelled hand proudly at the huge electric fan which turned above them. "I want you to use the finest, silk writing paper with our emblem on, your very best writing of course, Mendoza. No, make two copies, one for me to keep. When you have done it, bring them to me to sign before you go to deliver the best written one in person."

Frozen, Filipe Mendoza just bowed his head and said nothing. The ayah watched, a sudden gleam of understanding in her eye.

"You will take first bearer and second secretary. They must wear their finest livery and they will attend to you as my personal messenger and representative. You of course will wear your best European clothing. I will send for the derzi who will make up more European clothes for you. If you are to petition the governor, you must go very respectable, as my secretary. Tell him we do not ask for any aid from the British, our own funds will supply everything. But I must have Doctor Muir to advise me. He will know what to do, where to build and so forth." For just a moment, she paused, her face animated, her jewelled foot tapping. "You will drive to the train station in His Highness' small, fast car and you will travel first class as you are my representative." Seeing only a blank face before her, her tongue grew sharp. "Do you hear me, Mendoza?" He nodded and tried to clear his throat but she went on. "Send me the head gardener and the estate manager before you leave. I have work for them while you are away. Now go and write that letter, beautifully, while I arrange some gifts."

Filipe Mendoza felt as if a hurricane was whipping his heals as he fled to his little study at the back of the palace. On his way he gave instructions for the men who the rani wanted to see to attend her. The fine paper spread before him, he paused, giving himself the luxury of a few moments reverie. So she was better! So things would now begin to move again! Good, he thought, and dipped the pen into the inkwell.

CHAPTER EIGHT

LOVE

They returned two weeks later, the secretary, quiet as ever but with a glow of success on his face. The head bearer and second secretary on the other hand were grinning stupidly, supremely puffed up with pride having not only been, travelling first class, to the city, but to Government House.

Waving her dismissal at them, joyfully they sped to relate their experiences to one and all, and in doing so gained high kudos.

"So?" the rani did not waste words. Her secretary almost forgot himself and began to smile, but checked in time. Very seriously he told his employer all that had happened, how, after some delay they had been received, how, he and his colleagues had actually been given accommodation by Doctor Muir, in his own bungalow.

"I was given my own guest room highness, my colleagues had good quarters at the back. We could not have received kinder hospitality, if he had been a blood relative, highness. Every kindness was shown to me, a car put at my disposal for when I went to Government House. I have to tell you, Highness, that all together this was a most satisfactory excursion, most far seeing of you to arrange for us to go. A mere letter would certainly not have achieved such results." Then realizing he was talking too much he resumed his distant tactful attitude and finished with,

"Doctor Muir is hoping to come very soon."

Sushila felt her heart hammering.

"When?" she asked.

"Doctor Muir will be leaving India for good shortly, highness. He undertook to get three months leave before he goes, which he will spend here. He had many things to do, the packing up of his possessions, or the disposal of them. Hence he kept us some days, just to make sure. Before he comes he has to hand over his house and office to his successor and make arrangements for his property. He hopes to arrive before long with an architect friend of his, an Indian gentleman. So, highness," he finally allowed a proud smile to light on his face, "you have succeeded in the first step to create your hospital."

Sushila turned and gazed out of the tall window onto the dry lawns. He was coming, for three months. She felt her hands tremble so she clutched at them while her heart sang with joy.

"Now, Mendoza, I know you must be tired, but I will keep you for awhile longer. You have succeeded with the first step, now I want to show you what miracle I have also achieved in your absence in so little time. Come," ayah slipped on some slippers on the tiny feet and taking up an umbrella walked behind her mistress.

"Do not think that here we have been idle. You must see what I have been doing while you were away." She walked swiftly out to the back of the palace, across the great yards, through an arch into the bright, hot sunshine where she stopped and the secretary gazed about them in amazement. For where, surrounding a great courtyard had stood a huge stone barn and countless outbuildings, now were long rows of neatly stacked stone blocks. She turned, smiling at his astonished face.

"Time, and probably cost will be important. I hated these old buildings, of no use, dusty and full of scorpions and snakes. We have no need for stables now we have no elephants or horses. Those days are long past but the materials they were built of are of great worth and not least, will save much time and money. So now we at least have something to start with. I have ordered sand and cement, masons, workmen and carpenters, so the moment Doctor Muir arrives, they will be summoned to meet him. I have been around the estate and chosen two possible sites to build the hospital, but he and the architect must choose, for there is a good water supply at one, which is closer to the town, although the other site is larger."

Filipe Mendoza looked down at his little rani in admiration as he often would during the coming weeks and months. Never could he have thought it possible for a woman in her position to drive such a work force so successfully. It was a brilliant move on her part.

"Highness," Philip Mendoza actually smiled at his employer. "I am greatly impressed by your efforts, and in such a short time, greatly!" He realized he was speaking out of place but she smiled at him radiantly, her lovely dark eyes bright with some inner joy and so he went on. "You were so right to utilize those old buildings with their fine stone blocks, Doctor Muir will be so impressed too. Such a saving of time and money, which will also make handsome buildings, a brainwave indeed. Highness," he bowed, "I most sincerely and warmly congratulate you."

Sushila tuned on her sandaled feel but he caught a glimpse of her smile as she hurried away. So he had not spoken out of turn, he had warmed her heart. Happy himself he went outside once more, forgetting his fatigue and the searing heat with pad and pen to count and measure the neat rows of stone she had so cleverly organised. They would for sure be most useful as well as make a most handsome hospital.

It would be a great bonus to the area, they would no more be considered a backward little principality, without education or thought for the common people. What was more, the whispers would grow deafening, the project the talk of the town, small as it was, everyone vying with each other to produce and provide every assistance, without, hopefully, too much dishonesty. Undoubtedly one and all were delighted. Thus, which was not the normal way of things, all tasks, deliveries and difficulties were swept along and success was unusually swift and sweet. Hence greed and ambition were for once overtaken by optimism. The secretary breathed a deep sigh of satisfaction. The doctor sahib would be greatly surprised and pleased.

One more thing the rani organized. A pavilion for the doctor, near enough to the palace for her to see it, but far enough to give him privacy.

Once again the palace staff were goaded into action, the dusty lawn on which the pavilion would be situated was swept till bare. The glorious cloth pavilions, unused for years were brought out, shaken, sorted, till the rani chose one. A smallish tent it was, with two rooms, very beautiful, embroidered and colourful and then the palava of erecting it. All the while the little prince raced in and out joyfully, such excitement, for his friend, the Doctor Sahib would be coming.

"Electricity!" she exclaimed. So the electrician from town who had installed the palace electricity came and a long lead was carefully laid just under the surface of the lawn.

"Electric fans," she demanded, "lights." And everyone ran to do her bidding. "Beds, mosquito nets, furniture." Mendoza always with his pen and pad was beside her as they chose, carried, arranged and re-arranged. She fussed, she fumed if things did not work out as she wanted.

"The Indian architect gentleman must have a good desk for his papers in his room." A large desk was found.

"Call the man with the pet mongoose and tell him that he is to tour the garden every night till further notice. We cannot risk our guests being bitten by snakes!"

In a welcome lull, Filipe Mendoza chose his words carefully.

"Highess," she actually smiled up at him.

"What is it now, Mendoza?"

He coughed. "Perhaps an imposition Highness, perhaps not to your liking." She frowned.

"Speak man, for I do not understand what you are trying to say."

He coughed again. "Doctor Muir," another cough, "while I was at his bungalow," he hesitated then glimpsed his employer's face and hurried on. "Early every morning, a syce brought his horse and he rode out for about two hours before breakfast. It seemed to make him happy."

Sushila looked at him in astonishment then, her voice raised said,

"Then go to my first brother at once to find him a horse and a syce and go to ask him. Now!" Pondering on this new development, the rani added. "Go in the fast car and request this of him immediately. And tell him of our progress," she added as an afterthought.

Everything was ready. Perfection. Sushila saw to the flowers, for she remembered how the doctor had brought flowers in for the sick. Every night the mongoose man went around the palace beating his baton on trees to frighten the snakes. Secretly, the young prince placed some of his most precious toys in the doctor's room. The adults noted this, smiled and left them.

Two horses arrived and were put into good stables which had not been ripped down. Everyone ran, little tasks which had been done were done again. Everything was ready.

Thankfully they arrived at dusk so the pavilion was alight, as a fairy tale. And the reward was that on seeing it, Doctor Muir, clapped his hands and laughed with joy.

"Madam," he said in English, then in Hindi, "You have surpassed yourself. Bless you, it is enchanting, wonderful!" And laughed again. Then the little prince ran to him and he was picked up and swung around. It was a joyful scene.

The following morning early Sushila looked discretely out of her windows and saw the doctor sahib ride off on the great horse her brother had sent for him, the syce following behind. He looked so fine, and she must instruct the syce to guide him to the most beautiful areas so he could appreciate their country.

"We must leave space for future development, highness," said Doctor Muir. "Or, it is better to start small and grow according to your needs than to be too ambitious to start with." All this, albeit stumbling sometimes, in her own language. For he had learnt well, and it was her pleasure to gently correct him occasionally, for which he seemed more than grateful.

Early every day after his ride and bath, they met on the terrace with the head workmen. The doctor, the architect, the secretary and whoever else came, all looked to the beautiful little lady who held the reigns in her hands as well, it seemed, as a whip.

The rani nodded, smiled, ordered, demanded, scolded, even shouted at times and in astonishingly short time, had unprecedented cooperation. The Indian architect and Doctor Muir spent hours poring over plans, discussing with the rani, with the local medics, and with the town elders. Apparently everyone had their say, while scores of coolies laboured so that the foundations were dug, the walls went up, windows and doors went in, red roof tiles were laid, and marble floors stretched, cool and clean, throughout the fine, new hospital.

Despite the good feeling of progress and success, the evenings were the best time for the rani as all was quiet and everyone had left. There was no hammering or dust rising from down the hill, and the coolness of the night brought out the sweet scent of jasmine. So after the prince had some time for his hug, perhaps a story, it became their habit to sit quietly, talking over a light meal.

She always ordered the best food for him, not too chilly hot, to suit his European tastes and showing him that he was greatly appreciated in every way. It was so agreeable to watch him in the gloom, sitting with his legs stretched out on the long chairs smoking his pipe. Never in her life had she felt such peace and companionship. Consciously, she was aware of the first love she had ever felt for a man, that she must treasure every memory deep in her soul.

His very nearness sometimes made her feel faint and she longed for his touch. But all he did was to bow to her, eyes twinkling, perhaps taking her hand, before going off to his quarters in the garden.

It certainly was a great satisfaction to see the building progress. However, with the furious pace, the days flew past, and Sushila tried not to think of his leaving.

Before long it was time for the town photographer and the local press to be called in.

Demure in her white sari, Sushila stood seriously beside the tall foreigner while their photographs were taken. Then a chair was brought and she was seated, with the doctor and the architect behind her. Moved to another vantage point, together they stood, first just the rani with Doctor Muir, then, together with their closest staff. Eventually, a chaotic, noisy arrangement, the entire work force was preserved on celluloid for posterity. Never had such a small hospital had such a grand or appreciative opening with suitable fire crackers to ward off evil spirits. The local people peered, round-eyed, as many strangers came too, another doctor, some nurses, fearfully impressive in their white uniforms and saris. The local administrator came himself, together with his entourage, to officially open it, so inevitably there was a grand tamasha, a huge affair, a great success. It was all there in the photographs never to be forgotten.

"I will be very sad when you leave, Doctor," Sushila said, taking his hands in an uncharacteristic gesture. "This has been the finest, happiest time of my life. I am so proud. I am so grateful. Doctor Sahib, I so much hope that you will visit us again before too long." Yet while she spoke a knife turned in her breast and she wondered if he had any inkling of her pain, for it was so deep, surely as a doctor, he must see it? She also knew in her inner soul, that he would never return.

With a big smile the tall young foreigner, lifted her hand and kissed it. Struggling with his poor Hindi, he tried to tell her how much he had enjoyed his time with her, how proud he was of their success, how impressed he was by her courage and energy. He spoke softly, searching for the unusual words, understanding.

They sat on a veranda in the dusk, mosquito burners giving their distinctive smoky smell, curling from under their chairs. The rani drank her lime juice while the doctor drank his tall glass of iced whisky. It was so peaceful, with just the sounds of the night, Sushila wished this time would never end. The little raja came to say good bye, and clung to the tall now familiar man who hugged him.

"Exercise that leg, little highness," he whispered, "even when I am gone!" The boy hugged him fiercely trying not to cry.

Sushila closed her eyes, then blinked hard to make room for the tears which welled there. He was going, of course he was. She knew that. But her heart would break, for, she trembled, for the first time in her life, she knew what it was to love, to be in love. At no time had she indicated her feelings to him, timid, shy. Always she had been busy, hiding her feelings by bossily making sure things would be done, and as he liked, properly. Had that been foolish of her? At no time had he ever shown any disrespect to her, by word or deed. Oh, if only. Finally she rose, the night deep and a sliver of a moon just rising. She turned to him, and held out her hands. A tear trickled down a cheek, but she did not wipe it away and he saw it. Then, to her great surprise he drew her close and gently folded his arms about her, one hand softly caressing her head, speaking unintelligible words. Such peace, such security. So she let her tears fall wetting his jacket. Because he was leaving. For the hopelessness of her life. For the past lost and useless years and the endless lonely years which lay before her.

"Hush, little lady, hush," he said, rocking her. "You'll be alright, you are a fighter." Then he bent down to peer into her face in the darkness and taking out a white handkerchief, he gently wiped her eyes. Then he said, in her language, "Weep not, little queen, for you are so special, so good. You have made a miracle here for your people, you will be ever blessed. Your name and that of your family will stay high in the esteem of this town. Your actions have been perfect, fine, far reaching and, for myself, I will never forget you all my life," and held her close, gently rocking, once more. Slowly her shaking shoulders quietened and at last calm and still, she stood back a pace and gazed at her love for the last time. Pressing her hands together in farewell, she quietly turned and went into the palace where waiting in the shadows, her silent nurse took her by the hand and swiftly led her to the sanctuary of her own rooms.

That night, Filipe Mendoza joined the doctor in his tent and unusually took a whisky with him.

"Everyone will miss you doctor, particularly the rani and little rajah. You have filled their lives these months, indeed, all our lives. I," he added quietly, "am privileged to have served you too."

The young doctor looked at the quiet Anglo-Portuguese in surprise.

"I hope that you consider me a friend, Filipe, you have helped me beyond words, I could never, ever have managed without you. And if in the future there is anything I can do for you, do not hesitate to let me know." He handed him an envelope, "Where you can find me until I am settled." Then he frowned. "Now I have a favour to ask of you, Filipe, my servant, such a good man. He has been with me for three years and unfortunately my successor is bringing his own staff. Is it possible that the rani will employ him? He speaks English, is honest, and a clever worker. He even helped me occasionally with medical affairs." Filipe nodded.

"Yes I am sure she will, he can be helpful with the little prince, teach him some English, play games with him and so forth, which the other servants do not. They merely indulge him. Kindly tell him to be firm," he smiled, pleased. "A good idea sir. Now I thank you for your hospitality, your kindness to me, but as you are to leave early, you must get your sleep."

They shook hands warmly and went their ways.

CHAPTER NINE

KARRENDSKIS

"It was quite by chance that I was in the shop that day," my uncle Algie smiled brightly at me, "for as you know, I rarely go up to town nowadays, far too tiring. But I had an annual dinner, at the North India Club, you know I can't resist a curry. So stayed at the club and of course, I could not fail to call in at the old place." He took a sip of tea, silently approved and then another.

I always kept his favourite brew for him, for although he lives in our granny flat, being a very tactful man, he visits rarely. Having said that, it is we, who live in his house, the old place which luckily, the Karrendski grandparents had bought, in good times. Uncle Algie had organized the division, and handed the whole place over to us on condition that we looked after him in his dotage. As he is a poppet, we were the lucky ones.

At the moment I could see he was in top form, rather excited indeed, so made sure he knew I was all attention, for it was obvious he was full of news, with a capital N and wanted to talk.

"As usual, they gave me a warm welcome," he continued balancing his cup. "Nowadays, they do not suspect me of snooping, I really think it is genuine. Sadly, the stock isn't what it used to be, but then, it is a sign of the times. In my day things were so very different. We always had glorious pieces, ancient, fearfully rare and or valuable. Nowadays unfortunately, there is all too little of real worth. But, as in this case, many of our old customers, those who are still alive of course, do return to us." He shook his white head sadly, "Usually, they just come to sell their treasures, for

34

times are hard and so many of them live in sadly reduced circumstances." He emptied his cup and put it down. It really was a pleasure seeing him so excited, so I nodded at him in encouragement to go on with his story. This he did, yet being an old gentleman, it took about a year to all come out, and because it was so long and rambling, I decided to write it down in my diary, as it came, so I can remember.

At the beginning, I merely thought that this was an interesting tale about the purchase of some extraordinary piece of jewellery. But as the story unfolded, I gradually realized that although it certainly did have gems in it, basically it was in fact a most gentle and unusual love story, which originated in the North of India. That it took some extraordinary coincidences and very many years to blossom, is not so very strange. Except apparently, that it was all directed by astrology, from beginning to end.

My brother, Timothy, now runs the shop. He was a rather delicate child and took to the quiet life of jewels and clocks like a duck to water. Or maybe it was in his genes. Anyway, he and his wife live there, the upstairs apartment being quite the height of luxury compared to what it was. But perhaps this needs some of our family history for a start, because it is in a small way, part of it.

Uncle Algie and my mother Clarissa were the third and fourth children of Clara and Nicholas Karrendski. The story of their parent's meeting is also worth a mention, for Clara was the only child of the clock maker, Algernon Knowledge. (Such a strange name, we guessed there must have been a teacher somewhere amongst his ancestors.) Knowledges was a small jeweller and clock maker, tucked away on the corner of a mews near the park in the West End of London. So tucked away indeed, that theirs was not a thriving concern, just, without wishing to sound punnish, ticking over. My grandmother told me that they were just shutting up shop on a Saturday evening, when a knock brought in a strange, tall, thin young man. Very white and obviously utterly exhausted, he promptly fainted on their linoleum! Which is how, eventually, we came to have a Russian grandfather. It seemed they hurriedly finished shutting up and somehow managed to carry their visitor into the room behind the shop which was living room-cum-kitchen, where in the warmth and with my grandmother's care, he soon revived.

It was a fortuitous event for him and Clara, for he had not been successful in selling the jewels he carried, secreted all over his person, having been offered silly prices. And here was a chance for my grandmother, aged thirty and "on the shelf", at last to procure a husband. Apparently Nicholas, who was five years her junior, had undertaken to sell the jewels for a small percentage for various Russian émigrés who were "too shy" to do it themselves.

Probably Nicholas was just plain hungry, for life for poorer émigrés was hard. Clara, with a sound head on her shoulders, managed somehow to buy all the pieces by borrowing from a well-to-do aunt, and by paying for the jewels in monthly instalments, which seemed to satisfy everyone. It also meant that Nicholas became a regular visitor, happy to at least be able to take his grand friends regular payments which, of course, brought more sales. For here was a reliable jeweller situated in such a discreet place, they could also hire back their pieces, if by happy chance a court dinner came their way. A small sum would be deducted from the sale price, so it never felt painful. Unless of course the piece sold, but then there were always other ways, and for a small fee and with great discretion, other interesting pieces could be hired. Thankfully the Knowledges were always so obliging.

Three years after their first meeting, old Mr. Knowledge died leaving everything to his daughter. Clara now quickly proposed two things to Nicholas, marriage and a partnership in the business. She was a neat, small woman with fair hair and fine blue eyes, but otherwise was quite unremarkable in every way. But her mind! What she lacked in looks she made up for with brains. Sensibly, Nicholas accepted both, for life in London continued hard, and the little mews shop had become more of a home to him than his cold attic in Bayswater. Determined to do at least one thing properly, Nicholas arranged their marriage in the Russian Orthodox Church, which much impressed the few Knowledge relations who attended. The grateful émigrés undertook the reception in a magnificent drawing room in a borrowed mansion, which completed the affair, even if Clara had handed over considerable sums for the refreshments, footmen, waiters and flowers. It turned out to be a good investment, for the aunt to whom she was indebted was so thrilled with the event and to have so much to recount to all her dull old friends, that she cancelled the remainder of the debt as a wedding gift, as well as ultimately leaving her all to them in her will.

Clara and Nicholas went to Paris for their honeymoon. Part business, part pleasure of course, for here was another source of magnificent jewels, and Clara was a clever woman, never one to miss an opportunity. They barely met the French, so wrapped up were they in the whirl of Russian émigré life which was more mad and gay than in London. Clara blossomed at last, bought herself outrageous clothes and hats and revelled in her loss of spinsterhood and her new position. To his unconscious surprise and pleasure, Nicholas saw that his previously plain little wife was a real success with his old countrymen. Clara knew just how to charm when she wanted to, and charm she did. He also found that her quiet manners hid a hot passion, and he realized he had been lucky in his choice of wife.

Perhaps her wisest move however, was to arrange the complete redecoration of their premises during their absence. It was the one thing which Nicholas needed. To belong, to be one with, and of his new country, and to dismiss and forget occasional longings, for the old.

There it was in its glory, sparkling new, so on their return they sat for a full two minutes in the carriage, gazing at it raptly. The shop-front was now in darkest green paint, picked out in gold. Splendid above the window hung the sign, Knowledge and Karrendski. Perceptive Clara, for this was just what her husband needed and was indeed, the making of him. His pride, joy and gratitude were enormous; so was born our family and our family fortunes. Within the year Clara bore twin sons, dark handsome boys just like their father. When men, after dramatic army careers, one losing a leg, the other an eye, Uncles Nicholas and Alexander eventually opened the Paris and New York branches of Karrendski's. Clara's third and fourth children favoured her, being fair and blue-eyed. Having excelled in the war in intelligence with his fluent Russian, Uncle Algie took over the London shop when his parents died. His sister, Clarissa, helped with the accounts so it was truly a family affair.

Despite being entirely independent, the three Karrendski brothers and their heirs, still work closely together.

No auction house failed to send catalogues to the family. No auction of worth failed to have amongst their clientele, one of the handsome Karrendskis.

"It must be good," said the auctioneer aside to his assistant, "if he is here."

Despite war and hardship, the family quietly prospered delighting in their stock, ever reluctant to part with it.

CHAPTER TEN

THE LETTER

So it was that brother Tim showed Uncle Algie that morning's interesting letter, over coffee. And knowing Tim, it was deliberately done with ulterior motive. While not wanting to lose old customers, he none the less blanched at the idea of a long train journey. Not least of his thoughts, was curiosity.

"With two beautiful boxes with your name inside," he read it out. "I realized that my father must have bought the pieces for my mother, from you. Therefore, and on a different matter, I will be most grateful if you could visit us here."

Of course he remembered them, the Saint Austell Muirs. Uncle Algie had met the older and much respected Doctor Muir in India before the war. A neat feminine hand, he told me, ever observant, it was from the daughter who he supposed must be in her early sixties now, remembering her as a fair, jolly girl. He saw that the address was the same, except that now she appeared to live in one of the lodges. He spoke quietly to himself, "So I suppose the big house is a hotel, or school or some such." I watched him as his eyes glazed with remembering.

Dear Uncle Algie. Always so correct and fine, and such an old-fashioned gentleman. I remember how he told me years before, how he had fought his father over entering the family business. How his young years in the war had made him restless and yearn for a more exciting life. Yet after he did go into the firm, his natural love of beautiful things soon totally occupied him.

38

The letter requested a personal visit, which could only
The lady wished to sell something of particular value wi'
this was a quality Karrendski's was well known for.

In a repaint after the war, somehow the "Knowledge
off the sign over the shop, so it became just "Karrendskis" thereafter.

Despite his age, Uncle Algie remains in fine fettle, and the occasional jaunt seems indeed to put new life in him. He never married again after his young wife died, so when he retired, he divided the old house as I have said before, luckily sharing it with us. Properly packed up, I sent him off to the wilds of the West Country, to be met by a taxi which drove him to the lodge of the fine old house he had known in his younger days. Not much had changed since he had been there during the war, when the old manor house had been used as a military nursing home and the wounded young Algie had spent a time there being patched up. It had been run by Major-General Doctor Samuel Saint Austell Muir, who although merely an old acquaintance, had given him a warm welcome. Somewhat his senior, with his wife, Penelope and daughter, Madeline, they had made the nursing home much more homely by their presence.

Apparently Uncle Algie had met Doctor Muir at a great Do, which he called "a tamasha" in the North of India. They had accompanied the Governor in his large retinue of staff on one of those grand occasions which took place before the war. The hospitality had been lavish, with traditional rides on great elephants and tiger shoots. Uncle Algie had many rich memories stashed away which he recounted without much urging. As far as he could remember, Sam, as Doctor Muir was commonly known, had been a good friend of the maharaja's family for many years. On one grand shooting party, he had accompanied the area governor as the medic. When the party left, he had remained behind at special request, to help set up a small hospital for the maharaja, or rather, the maharani, his formidable grandmother.

So now the story changes from our family to the Muirs. They and Uncle Algie remained casually in touch over the years. Sam had married Penelope Quinton, but had continued in the army until his retirement. When he retired from active service, he lived with his wife in her parent's fine old house in the West Country, for she did not care for foreign postings. They had only one child, a daughter, Madeline.

After the war, as a result of his friendship with the maharani, he suddenly found himself entrusted with the young son of the royal house in 1946. The poor lad had suffered a crippling polio, when a small child, leaving him somewhat lame, not at all what the maharani wanted. So, the boy was sent to England the moment there was civilian travel, for a miracle

. With him came the servant of Doctor Muir who had remained with
e Rani after he left. This loyal retainer smoothed out problems with the
boy and of course was delighted to be with his old master again. Gradually
the loyal servant understood that all that was being done for his little prince,
was for his own good. Of course it was essential that the boy did not lose
his mother tongue, yet at the beginning, there were many difficulties and it
was hard to get him to even try to speak English.

The young Madeline, all of six years old, had adored her new "brother"
on sight. She was taller and more robust than the young raja for some years.
He was at first, a small, slender, light-brown boy with strange pale-grey
eyes.

"From Persian stock no doubt," her father had told her.

While Madeline was lively and full of energy, the little raja arrived a
withdrawn, fearful little person, having been over cosseted by his loving
grandmother and all the servants. But not for long.

A bicycle was bought, one pedal removed, and the two children were
told to "GO"! Roger, as he soon became known, was furious. Obviously
very spoilt, he raged at his one-pedalled bike, threw it down, bit and kicked
it, but to no avail. Very quietly and firmly Doctor Muir explained in his own
language, his reasons. He must exercise the weak leg, the one-pedalled bike
would help re-build his muscles. Finally it was understood that he must
make the effort with his poor thin leg, to push himself up hill and down
dale.

He was also obliged, amidst fearful screams, to learn to swim in the icy
sea, which when he had, he excelled in and loved passionately. Another
indignity appeared. A long rope was tied into a great tree and Roger was
hung by the lame leg to it and swung mightily. The first time this happened,
breathless with terror, the little raja bit the doctor as he untied the soft
straps from his ankle, so got his very first spanking. Of course Madeline
insisted that she too must be swung and wildly enjoyed it making a fearful
noise but it did encourage the boy to see a mere girl, younger than he, flying
aloft.

Slowly, slowly, it began to work, both the exercises and the discipline.
The leg was never completely whole, but the limp was so slight eventually,
it was barely noticeable. Before long, mostly thanks to his adoring foster-
sister, Roger did become a happy boy, indeed quite a different young
person as he competed in school with the village kids. In his teens he shot
up, well overtaking his foster-sister in height, and grew into a surprisingly
tall and very handsome young man.

So when Uncle Algie visited them in the lodge, the story came out in dribs and drabs as the three of them sat chatting in the small sitting room. It was so cosy and comfortable, drinking out of porcelain cups, the finest tea, sent fresh from India of course. No mention was made that first day, as to why they had invited him. After reminiscing, they persuaded Uncle Algie to stay, and this became the pattern for his many future visits. To his astonishment he found that Roger was the cook, while Madeline laid the table, cleared and washed up. They laughed heartily at his surprise.

"I stuck Maddy's cooking for a week," said Roger grinning proudly, "then I took over. I phoned my daughter in India for recipes, and she soon began sending us foodstuffs, spices and so forth, which were fun experimenting with. We take the bus which passes the door to town twice a week, and go out to lunch. Generally we return by taxi, loaded down with our shopping. We might be invited out too, Sundays are always in the big house with Jim, Maddy's son, so it is only three or four days hard labour, which we enjoy. We put quite a lot of thought into it too, indeed we have become so cocky, we even invite people over, so we keep busy." They smiled warmly at each other.

His English, so Uncle Algie said, was perfect. Not a wisp or trace of the gentle sing-song of Indian English, due of course to his English education.

Having arrived in England in 1946, Roger started off in the village school with Madeline. Then, he went to a prep school nearby and later was educated in one of the finest public schools in the land. At university, he achieved a very good degree in law and then, sadly and with deep reluctance, his foster-father persuaded him to return to his own country.

"You have so much to offer your own country now, my boy. It needs you. We will always be here for you, but now, you have a debt to pay. Go home, son, learn about your own roots, and give your excellent grandmother the satisfaction of seeing and enjoying the fruits of her labours before she dies. For I am certain it was entirely due to her that you have stayed here and become such a success. You truly are a son to be proud of. Much as I hate the idea of your leaving and not having you about, it is the right thing to do."

Travel in the early years, had been tiresome, and being the only child, Roger had visited his home country but rarely. Each time he returned, he had brought sumptuous gifts for his "English family". The little lodge had much evidence of this, proudly filled with fine rugs and carvings, little silver dishes on little tables made of rosewood, teak or walnut.

"Father accepted money for his fees, nothing else," said Madeline. "Roger's grandmother was always sending wildly exotic things, but which my parents had to accept. The really special thing they did accept on my behalf, is my work box." She patted a sturdy, heavily carved little chest beside her. "See," she drew her finger over the carving, "these are my initials, Indian style. We always suspected that the tools inside, scissors, thimble, bobbins and so on, are pure gold, but we never checked. Better not to know! It is a wonderful old friend to me," she smoothed her hand over it again, "and I use it almost every day."

Back in India, much had changed with the young raja's family inheritance. After the British left, partition produced its own problems. Very little was left of the former, luxurious days, and the life he remembered as a young child was no more. Although both his parents had died, yet the old rani still hung on, for, he told them, he was quite sure, him alone. After more years at a college in North India, where he learnt everything about his native land which he should know, he joined a law firm. Madeline took up the story.

"We missed him dreadfully. For as you know, letters, phone calls and air flights in those days were nowhere as they are now. At some point Daddy suggested that as he had spent so many years in Britain, he might like to take dual nationality. I am not quite sure how it happened, but, on one of his visits, my parents formally adopted him, although by then, he was quite grown up. Having had him since he was nine, Daddy must have pulled some strings, for suddenly he was British, and he was Roger St. Austell Muir, or as we liked to tease him, RAM!" They laughed merrily.

He had returned to India to very little, for the family palaces and estates had all been confiscated by the state, yet as he was an only child, he had more than enough to live on, practising law. Somehow, his grandmother had retained property which had come from her family, and their lives were quietly prosperous.

As the years went by, both Madeline and Roger had married and had children. Roger visited England twice in the thirty odd years he was away, but Madeline never went out to India despite many intentions to do so. They wrote to each other every month, Roger craving family and the village news of his old home, while Madeline loved to hear all about the "romance of the East".

Suddenly they grinned at each other, then burst out laughing again.

"I'll have to tell him Roge," giggled Madeline.

"No! I will."

So in fits and starts they both told Uncle Algie about THE LETTERS.

"I was always so busy," mourned Roger. "For before I could turn around, I was an over-worked judge. Maddy's letters were the highlight of my month, and they were such good letters too, full of batty news of all the goings on here. I read and re-read them, indeed I have them all, forty odd years of letters. But what could I reply? Who would want to hear of my tedious work except the newspapers? I might have had a particularly gruesome case on hand, where a man had put three wives into a well before he was found out by the forth, who survived? I was going North to attend a land dispute at my old home? She had never been there. A disgruntled client had tried to kill me with a paper knife? Oh no, it was all too tedious." He sighed, his eyes had their far away look.

"My wife had been chosen by my grandmother before she died, a sweet girl, but traditional, so there was not much about the home to interest Maddy except perhaps the birth of my three children. At one point I dug out some fascinating old diaries of my father, and I asked an old clerk to translate them for me. Then it occurred to me that they were all far more interesting than my humdrum life, so I took to writing my few lines at the top of the letter on my little portable typewriter, and asked the clerk to fill in two more pages from the diaries before signing them. Without, as you will have gathered and I am very ashamed to say, first reading them!"

Once again they laughed, tears in their eyes, it was infectious.

"It took me quite a long time to work it out," Madeline continued. "Oh it was all great stuff with hunts and howdahs and great religious festivals and public hangings. None of it sounded at all familiar, so at first I thought that Roge was enjoying a new and exciting life which he wanted to share with me." She dabbed her eyes. "Then the clerk can't have been concentrating very well for events occurred which surely had been way in the past. My husband was something of a historian so he did a little research, and to our amusement, we concluded the truth. I held my tongue, or hand as it was, and just kept writing, and on receiving his splendid letters, every time, we had a good laugh."

"And when did you take him to task over it?" asked Uncle Algie.

Again they smiled warmly at each other.

"Oh ages later, when Maddy finally came out to visit me recently," Roger said gently. "Both our spouses had died, we had no ties, Maddy had some money from her share of the big house which as you know is now a nursing home. There was no excuse any more, it was so exciting. When at last she came out, I stopped writing of course, and she told me how much she missed my letters. At first I wondered at that wicked grin, then, of course, it all came out. Despite our hilarity, I was so ashamed, but she forgave me and forbade me to reprimand that moron clerk!"

"But," the charming Madeline took over again, "it was really such a good thing in the end." She looked smug. "For the clerk was so old, he needed that little job and paltry income to survive, so I asked him to translate the diaries, which he has done beautifully, for me and for posterity."

She rose and went to a desk and brought out a folder.

"You may be interested to browse through them, Algie. I'll put them in your room, so that you too can have a good laugh." She glanced fondly at Roger. "What happy chance that you were so busy dearest, otherwise they might well have been lost for all time. For they are indeed fascinating, and who knows, they may one day make a fine book, or at least go into some archives, for they really are of great historical interest and should be preserved."

CHAPTER ELEVEN

THE JOURNEY

Madeline had looked out of the plane's little window, down, down, where there seemed only mile upon mile of brown desert. The little quiver of excitement filled her again, despite her tiredness. Nervousness too, because she hadn't seen Roger for about ten years, and anyway, she didn't like flying. Previously, she had merely flown for an hour or two. This was different, a long journey. Then she smiled to herself. How silly she was being. Of course everything would be alright, a dream come true. How lucky she was to at last be going to see Roger in his own country, to stay with him in his home.

A pretty hostess bent over her and asked if she would like a drink. The plane was not full and there was a relaxed air about them. An orange juice soon was set on her tray, and Madeline murmured her thanks and looked down again.

Were people down there? Was there life, water? It was so strange, so foreign, she had no answer. Earlier, the head steward had brought her a note, a beam on his face. She touched it in her pocket, bless him, it merely said,

"Longing to see you, dearest sister, everything is ready for you."

It seemed that he was an important judge, very important, yet she could only think of him as Roge, her adopted brother, brother of her heart.

At Bombay, one of Roger's daughter's had met her. It had been decided she must break her journey to meet the rest of the family. It had been a joyful reunion for of course Lucky, as she was called, had stayed with her in

England when she was young. With great understanding Lucky had gently persuaded her to take a light meal, a shower, then put her to bed, their roles reversed. Her home was outside the city, a fine old house in a walled garden filled with colourful and scented flowers and Madeline closed her eyes and listened to the strange bird-song.

With a curious sense of unreality, still tired from her flight, she met Roger's grandchildren and son-in-law. The children received the board games she unpacked for them with wide and shining eyes. Weary though she was, she played with them, telling them of her childhood when their grandfather and she had played together and battled noisily.

Two days later she was back at the airport this time taking a smaller plane south. She felt rested, although the heat was fearsome. Once again they were up in the air, high above the huge tracts of India, and once again Madeline felt the quiver of fear and excitement at the unknown. The journey was dreadful. They rocked and bumped through the heat pockets and Madeline tried to still her stomach while an anxious steward hovered nearby.

At last they landed, and for a moment Madeline sat taking deep breaths of apprehension, dabbing at her nose with her powder puff. It was as if the red carpet was laid out for her yet again, for she was helped down the stairs, across the hot Tarmac and into the cool building where she shut her eyes for a moment to adjust to the dimness. A slight, older lady in blue, her blonde hair now almost silver, she gazed about at the mass of humanity searching for the tall, familiar figure.

"Maddy!" Roger hugged her, kissing her on both cheeks. She looked at him carefully, this dear, lanky man with a mop of silver hair, grey eyes bright with emotion. He was really unchanged, so familiar, just, as was she, a few years older.

"Dearest Roge," she felt a tear threaten and blinked hard. "So here I am at last!"

Then his son and other daughter came forward, their spouses and children, all demanding to be kissed by their English aunty. Suddenly she felt the tension go. Somehow the ice was broken with the love and laughter of welcome from her Indian family.

There was a family dinner that night at Roger's son's house. His other daughter, son-in-law and children and many other relatives were there, and she was quite surprised, having understood that they were Northern people.

"Oh be sure there are plenty more in the North," Roger laughed. "My children have married into huge families, so even if I was an only son, they are happily making up for it."

They sat in a cool courtyard where the scent of jasmine filled the air. Little mosquito coils were set under their chairs, being regularly attended by a uniformed butler who padded silently about amongst them on bare feet. They drank cold, fresh lime juice and conversed quietly, easily.

Madeline seemed still to hear the plane's engines somewhere in her head. She was tired and while they were driven back to Roger's house, she held his hand for reassurance.

"I can't really believe I am actually here, dearest."

"Well you can't imagine how happy I am to have you here after all these years." He frowned in the darkness of the car as the flashing lights of the city were left behind. "I do hope that you will be comfortable. My daughter has been toiling for weeks on your quarters in order that you will feel at home."

It took a couple of days for Madeline to settle in and enjoy all that had been prepared for her. Roger's house was a long, low bungalow in a big, walled garden which was full of flowers, the lawns being carefully tended. Her room led off a large central sitting room, and she had her own bathroom and veranda overlooking the garden. An older woman, called ayah, was to attend her and, although surprised, Madeline soon appreciated her constant kindness. Her clothes were unpacked and laundered. Her hair brush and few cosmetics were neatly laid out on the dressing table. Even her little watercolour paint box, pad and brushes were set on a table ready for her, should she have the inspiration to paint.

"It might be better if I put the air conditioning on a time switch Maddy," Roger fussed about. "It can be quite chilly in the early hours and the noise may disturb you. You will have to be careful not to catch a cold by going in and out of air-conditioned rooms, so many visitors do."

It was a charming room, with a large bed over which was draped a mosquito net. The furniture was handsome, solid, old and well polished. Everywhere she looked there were reminders of home. Photographs of them all together. Roger in his first school uniform. Mother and Dad at his prize giving. She knew them all of course, yet was touched by his display of his childhood life.

Servants silently came and went, always at attention for anything she needed. A flask of water was put on her bedside every day, a glass beside it covered with a beaded net. Flowers filled the air with their scent. The bowl of fruit was constantly re-filled. And all the while Madeline was aware that she was being very carefully scrutinised.

It took some days before she really felt herself again. Well it had been quite a journey and she was no longer a spring chicken. Her adopted niece and nephew called most days, often bringing their families and friends to meet her. Two more sets of board games were unpacked and received with delight and the children played out on the veranda giving the adults some quiet in which to talk.

Roger's lovely young women often called and took her shopping and she felt very privileged, suddenly and unexpectedly, the honoured lady. Together they bought her two saris, taught her how to put them on, dressed her, and it seemed spent a whole day happily taking lots of photographs.

Madeline had known that Roger was an important man, but was just a little surprised that his position resulted in her being utterly indulged in every way by rich and poor alike. Whatever she asked to do or see, it was immediately arranged.

"When may I attend court, Roge?" she asked one day.

He looked surprised. "You want to?" he asked unnecessarily.

She put on one of her familiar deep blue dresses, rather long with three-quarter sleeves as befitted an older lady and was driven to the court and quietly shown in halfway through the proceedings so as not to cause a disturbance. She had known that Roger was a high judge, was sure that he was to be trusted not to take bribes as some did, but now she watched with pride as obviously he was greatly respected.

Days and weeks passed and she grew familiar with Roger's home and family. The pace was gentle and she soon came to understand the climate and how not to get too hot and exhausted.

Roger was to be sixty five and soon to retire, and he seemed more busy than ever attending farewell functions. The family put on a splendid dinner party for his birthday and Madeline even baked his favourite chocolate cake for him after his daughter had hurriedly brought a small electric cooker. When Madeline first saw the kitchen, which was not joined to the house but was some way out in the garden, she had been amazed by it.

"Against fire, Maddy," Roger explained, "for this is an old house, and my servants have been with me for years, they do not care for change. As soon as you leave, the cooker will be covered with a dust cloth and won't be used until you come again!" They both laughed. "The cook likes his charcoal stove, he is used to it, and you have seen how well he copes with it. My daughter urges me to move into a flat in the city. She feels that this old house is not fit for me any more. But I love it, and could always really relax after work, without the rush and roar of the city, even if it is a little drive."

"What will happen to it when you retire, will you keep it?"

Roger nodded, "Of course, the servants are old too, I cannot turn them out. So wherever I travel to, I will return and meanwhile, they will care and guard it, while not having me to look after."

"Don't they have homes of their own?"

"But of course they do, yet," he smiled happily at her, "this is their home too. They feel safe here. They will have small pensions, but, theirs is a wonderful loyalty and I am very lucky to have them. Besides," he grew serious. "My children grew up here, it is their place too, and who knows, after I'm gone, one of them might like to retire here when their day comes."

At last the final court case was heard and dealt with. There seemed to be endless parties, the farewells were said with fine speeches and much garland giving, and so many gifts, there seemed no room to house them all.

"During all my working years," Roger idly inspected an elaborate silver dish amongst the presents, "I never accepted gifts." He put the dish down. "No, that is not true, I did accept eatables, fruit and vegetables, at feast days I would accept a turkey or two. But valuables, never. Far too risky to get embroiled in corruption, and although it was not understood for a long time, they came to accept that it was my way and due to my English education."

Madeline was intrigued. "You mean people would give you expensive gifts in order to sway a judgment?"

Roger laughed. "You hit the nail on the head. My wife used to rage at me for not accepting the many pretty, precious things which came our way. I had to be very strict with her. Enjoy them for two days, I would say, for then they are going back! Pity she isn't here to meet you and to enjoy at last the fruits of my labours."

The plan was that they were to travel to the North, to see Roger's old family estates, those magical places which Madeline knew about so intimately from her own father and from the letters taken from Roger's father's diaries.

"We will stay in the loveliest palace which is now a government run hotel. I was born there and lived there until I came to you. Then later when I returned, I was at college in that area and stayed there but as a guest, for as you know, it was all confiscated, although I did get some compensation with which I bought this house. I have registered as Roger Muir!" he laughed, "I am hoping that it might save us a little trouble and as it is years since I have been there, certainly no one will recognise me."

Madeline found that the leave-taking from family, friends and servants was surprisingly touching.

"Promise you will come back aunty!" Roger's daughter implored her, eyes brimming with tears. "Now that we all know you and see that you are really our aunty, promise you will return?"

Madeline promised, almost as tearfully, that of course she would come back, nothing could keep her away.

CHAPTER TWELVE

THE NORTH

The journey north seemed far easier than when she had arrived and travelled south. It might have been because now Roger saw to everything with extreme ease, or that she was so rested. Once again they stayed with Roger's elder daughter in Bombay for some days, then they continued their journey by train. Madeline never tired of gazing out of the window as the world flew by. They had decided that it would be fun travelling by train instead of plane, and they both enjoyed it. A huge train, they had their own first class carriage and Madeline found it all a wonderful adventure.

When they arrived at their destination, they were met and driven by car until the hills rose ahead of them and the air grew thinner and cooler. Now, very often, Roger leant forward and delighted in pointing out many familiar sights.

Just as the sun was setting, they saw ahead of them a fairy tale palace, and Madeline strained forward, eyes wide.

"Crafty old thing," she said, grinning at him, "you arranged that we should arrive at this time so that I would see it at its best." Roger gave her an arch smile and told the driver to stop so they could get out and stretch their legs.

Even out of the air-conditioned car, Madeline found with relief, it was much cooler. She gazed at the golden palace in the distance, the setting sun giving it a rosy glow. It was as in a story book. Beautifully carved, latticed stone decorations adorned every surface, while graceful great trees framed it as in a picture.

"It is lovely, Roge dear, exquisite. How on earth did you cope with our funny old house and the cold climate of England after growing up here?"

"Only till I was nine, Maddy. And of course being a child I took everything here for granted. My new home and country on the other hand were exciting, not," he added gaily, "forgetting the bike!" And laughed taking her arm, led her back to the car.

As they entered the wide gates, the freshness of the tended garden surrounded them. Sweeping to a halt in front of fine stone steps, they paused for a moment, and Madeline gazed about raptly. What a lovely place.

A liveried servant ran out to open the car door, followed by a smart young man who introduced himself as the assistant manager. "Welcome Sir, welcome Madam!"

They followed him as their luggage was carried up the wide curving stairs and disappeared. While Roger filled in the visitors' book, he seemed barely to be concentrating, so busy was he gazing about him.

"Lovely!" breathed Madeline, which brought her a fleeting sweet smile.

Their suite was splendid, huge, high-ceilinged and perfectly arranged. There was a central sitting room with a bedroom on either side each with a bathroom off. From all the rooms they stepped onto a long, connecting balcony filled with flowers in pots and festooned with flowering creepers.

"A shower first my dear, don't you think? Then perhaps you would like to go down to the dining room, or maybe you would prefer to eat up here?"

"Oh, Roge," Madeline stood in the centre of their gracious sitting room. "What a perfect ending to a wonderful holiday! To actually spend one month in your old home! I shall be able to think about it when I am back in my little lodge. But oh!" She turned to face him, her face quite stricken with pain. "I shall miss you so much."

He quickly took her hands. "Darling girl. Do not get upset, we have days yet, days after lovely days. And you will return, I am quite sure. This is just the first of many visits, you will see."

Yet a strange little pain had settled in Madeline's stomach. She really hadn't been aware how lonely she had been, but now she realized that she had. Now, after weeks of Roger's familiar and delightful company, she felt a new woman, bright and optimistic. Forcing a smile, she gave him a peck on the cheek and went to shower and change, trying not to think of how soon she would be flying home.

It seemed as if nothing was too much trouble for the staff, and they were hovered over and looked after, every request immediately granted.

It was all truly magical and so spacious, that the few other residents did not seem to intrude. Madeline gazed around while they sauntered through the public rooms and the gardens while Roger told her what they had been, who had slept there, how the fountain worked. She did ask occasional questions, but on the whole she just waited for Roger to tell her. It seemed that the memories flooded back, for as they strolled arm in arm or wandered in the shaded walks away from the other guests, all the while, Roger remembered.

There was an older English couple amongst the guests who kept very much to themselves. Madeline had overheard the elderly man being called "Brigadier", who kept glancing at her, with she realized, disapproval.

So, she thought, you criticize me because I am with my beloved Roger, and you feel that as we are of different race and colour, I am letting the side down. Well! With a slight bow of her head she smiled at them and said kindly, "Good evening."

Every early morning and late evening they wandered further into the park, somehow never being short of things to speak about. He showed her the old stables, the area where the ponies and elephants had been housed. Much was in decay the further they went from the hotel, but it seemed that every place even now had a purpose.

Suddenly on one of these saunters an old gardener stopped directly in front of them. He bowed low, fell on his knees salaaming and muttering, "Sahib, chota Sahib." Roger went to raise him up, no easy feat as he seemed so frail.

Madeline was alarmed, "What is he saying Roge?"

The old man on his feet again, Roger held his hands firmly and spoke quickly and quietly to him. It was difficult to get away, with tears streaming down his face, the old gardener held on tightly.

"He remembers me, can you believe it? I am still the little master to him. He was a gardener's boy when I was a kid, and blow me, here he still is."

One of the hotel staff appeared as if by magic and began remonstrating with the old man, but yet again Roger spoke in a quiet yet firm voice and made peace.

After that, they seemed to meet the old gardener whenever they walked in the early mornings or cool evenings and inevitably he had some small gift of flowers or fruit to press into their hands. When Roger was out, Madeline made a point of strolling in the grounds till she met the old man. Of course she understood not a word that he was saying, no doubt he did not understand her either. Yet happily there was a mutual understanding, and it was so pleasant to have found a friend, which gave her a warm feeling.

At last she felt inspired to paint, and taking the exotic flowers given by the old gardener, she began tentatively to experiment. Gaining confidence, her little pad began to store memories to take home. It was the perfect, quiet pastime to occupy herself when Roger was out. For, he told her, he had an agent caring for his grandmother's properties, and he had much business to discuss over them.

Having given the old gardener the first painting she was satisfied with, she glowed with his delight and apparent praise. Naturally it prompted him to produce even more perfect specimens for her to paint. It kept her happily busy.

Occasionally they drove into the little town nearby and Madeline sauntered in the bazaar escorted by their driver while Roger did some business. It was all so fascinating, the variety of goods on display, the smells, the colour, and in that comparatively rich area, the beautifully dressed and bejewelled country women who brought in their wares from the villages. Some days they drove far out into the hills, called on old acquaintances or explored ancient ruins and graveyards. The days passed easily and Madeline couldn't remember when she had been so utterly contented.

After dinner one day they were sitting out on their veranda when they were alerted by a noisy cavalcade of jeeps arriving. There seemed to be some commotion and Madeline leant over the stone balcony to see what was going on. A tall, handsome and very smartly uniformed policeman was being greeted by the manager, then, two at a time, climbed the steps into the hotel.

Moments later a servant knocked discretely, and offered Roger a tray with a note on it. Frowning in the dimming light, Roger's face looked serious.

"Something is up, Maddy my love. I do hope they aren't going to involve me in some nasty case now. I am retired damn it! Will you stay here or come down with me."

Madeline thought for a brief moment. "I didn't come here to miss out on anything," she retorted rising, and gathering her stole about her. "Certainly I am coming down."

There was an expectant hush in the wide entrance hall, several uniformed policemen stood about and it was obvious that the staff were rather nervous.

Roger walked in front of her down the gracious stairs and the tall policeman, very well turned out in his finest, came forward to meet him. Suddenly both men burst out laughing and clasped hands, then embraced roughly, apparently old friends. Little words drifted up to where Madeline stood watching, still on the stairs. "You old dog!" and "My but you have grown" and so forth.

"My sister," Roger turned and held a hand out to Madeline, "remember I told you all about her?" Madeline smiled up into a handsome bearded face where grey eyes surveyed her. "Maddy, meet my old friend, Dee, from college days. Call him Dee, for you'd never be able to pronounce his name."

Courtesies done with, they walked up to their suite again where Madeline soon excused herself in order to leave the men by themselves.

Laughing, talking non-stop, the two old friends sat up late catching up on their news. The smell of cheroots, mosquito coils and jasmine drifted through the veranda doors and Madeline lay under her mosquito net contentedly sleepy, half listening.

Roger was in a very jolly mood the following day and excused himself to go off to see his friend so Madeline stayed in the hotel, painted and enjoyed a quiet day.

At lunch, the English lady stopped by her table and murmured, "No trouble I hope?"

Madeline was rather surprised and it took a moment for her to understand what the woman was getting at. Then she laughed lightly. "No indeed," she replied kindly, "my brother is from here, and that was an old college friend. They are spending the day together, no doubt catching up on old times."

The woman looked at her most oddly, eyes wide, nodded slightly and went on to her table where the brigadier waited for her. Several times during the meal Madeline was aware of their scrutiny and smiled into her plate. They must be imagining all sorts of lurid stories from her referring to Roger as her brother. Ah, well, let them, she thought, stuffy unfriendly lot.

The next day Roger showed Madeline a fine big announcement on the hotel notice board. It read,

"Volunteers needed to make up a team to play cricket against Saint Mathew's College next Saturday. Whites and all equipment will be supplied. Recruits please meet on the front lawn at 5 pm tomorrow evening. Sign below. Gentlemen Only Please!"

Madeline burst out laughing. "And what do you mean by Gentlemen Only Please?"

"Just what I say, woman! I remember well what a terrific bowler you were, and of course, it just can't be allowed here, we men might lose face.

Now, let us see if we have any takers. We've already eight, so we might make it."

CHAPTER THIRTEEN

BREAKING THE ICE

Now every hour seemed to be full of the cricket match. They went to the college and while Roger discussed arrangements, Madeline was shown around by two delightful young students. They answered her questions most carefully, and asked two to her one, their eyes bright with enthusiasm. It was a charming building, very gracious and airy with verandas all around it in the old colonial style. The grounds were meticulously kept, with great shady trees, lawns and flower beds. The tennis courts and games fields were obviously much in use and Madeline considered them very lucky young men, with which they agreed.

That evening, a tailor arrived at the hotel with a boy in tow, well draped with a selection of whites for Roger to try on. Speedily putting pins in here and there, the tailor assured Roger that they would be ready the next day.

Seeing Madeline's face, Roger laughed out loud. "A little different from Mrs. Clark, eh?"

Remembering how in the days of clothes rationing, he'd had so many of his foster father's hand-me-downs altered. Madeline gave him a mock scowl. "Father's good tweeds were a lot more work to alter than cotton whites!"

They now had nine in their team and Roger had begun to fret. "There surely must be a couple of old boys somewhere about we can rope in." So off he went in search of them leaving Madeline to wander once more in the glorious gardens. Never had she seen such impressive trees and shrubs. The colours and the scents were spectacular. Carefully placing herself to the best advantage, she tried to take good shots of exotic blooms with her small camera, for even with her little paintings, surely no one would believe her descriptions when she got home.

Then, in a patch of shade around a bend, she was startled to come upon the old gardener sitting on the bare earth, his face twisted in pain while he nursed his leg.

"Oh my dear," Madeline fell to her knees beside him. "What is it? What happened?"

The old man tried to speak, but his mouth seemed unable to work. Then he made an action with a hand, a twisting, moving action which Madeline immediately understood described a snake. Startled, she sympathetically rested her hand on his shoulder, then jumped up and ran back to the hotel. As she passed a veranda where the brigadier's wife was sitting, she breathlessly called out. "The old gardener has been bitten by a snake," and ran on.

There seemed nobody about, it still being afternoon, a lull in the day, so Madeline ran around to the back of the hotel and asked a sleepy boy for help. Obviously her anxiety was very apparent because before long, her driver appeared, hastily pulling on his jacket. Somehow they got the old man into the car and with the driver, the brigadier's wife and Madeline, they raced the short distance to the hospital which having passed by it every day, they now knew well. No sooner had they screeched to a halt in front of the emergency entrance, a stretcher appeared and the old man disappeared into the cool dimness of the hospital.

Madeline sat down in the shade on a stone bench outside feeling hot and distressed.

The brigadier's wife took out a small phial from her bag and sprinkled a hanky with it.

"Here," she said, sitting beside her, "some good old English lavender should soothe you. I'm Mary Burroughs," she said, "of course there had to be a crisis for us to introduce ourselves, and I know," she added kindly, "that you are Madeline Eliot." Madeline sniffed the proffered hanky gratefully and was horrified to find that she was trembling.

"That is better now, Madeline, we'll just rest here for a while. I was a nurse in my far and distant past and realize that the old man was very cold and shocked. So I hope that he was able to tell them what it was that bit him."

The driver hovered and Madeline beckoned to him. "Thank you so much, now do go back to the hotel. If you see sahib, please tell him we are here and that we will walk back as it gets cooler." Then turning to her new friend for affirmation said, "I think we'd both rather find out how the old man fares. I have become rather fond of him, and I know Roger is, he knew him as a child." Saluting as was his habit, the driver drove off.

It was surprisingly pleasant in the shade of the veranda despite the blinding white of the walls. Madeline tried to steady her breath and watched as people came and went. Then, some time later, an orderly approached them, who they recognised as one of the stretcher bearers.

"Will Madams come in please? I take you to the director."

They followed him and were shown into an airy office where a white coated doctor sat. He rose, smiling, and extended his hand.

"Doctor Chandra, ladies. I have to thank you for bringing in the old man. He told us it was a cobra, one he has been after for a long time, the old fool!"

The orderly hovered and an order was rapped out, so he disappeared.

"I understand that you are staying in The Palace Hotel, very nice, especially at this time of year." The orderly re-appeared in record time carrying a tray on which sat three frosted glasses of lime juice. "Help yourselves please ladies, I see that you have both had a bit of a shock too. It will revive you. Don't worry, he will be alright, he is a tough old fellow that one. This isn't the first time he has been here."

Gratefully Madeline drank her juice and realized that yes, she had been shocked. She smiled at the doctor. "Thank you so much, doctor. At my age, I rarely run as I did then, and this is perfect," she drank again, and repeated herself trying to steady her hand, "thank you so much."

Then she sat back in her chair and listened idly as Mary Burroughs talked with the doctor about her training, many years previously in a big London hospital. He told them that he had also trained in Britain, but in Edinburgh and what a happy time he had had there as a young man.

Madeline was gazing about the room which was hung with photographs of many years. Then she got up and walked to see them more clearly, still nursing her cold drink.

"Doctor Chandra," she touched a large and yellowed photograph. "I do believe that this is my father, Doctor Saint Austell Muir, when he was a very young man!"

Oh, the coincidences of life! What a joy to be sitting in the very hospital which he had helped to build so many years before. The doctor was surprised and delighted and together they gazed at the photograph of a tall, young man in uniform, standing beside a beautiful, small Indian lady.

"She," the doctor explained, "was the maharani who was our benefactor. A far-sighted lady, it was she who enlisted the help of the British authorities and your father, oh so many years ago, to build this hospital. It seems that your father and she got along very well, for according to rumour, she did not, as was her habit, argue with him at all. Thanks to them, this small town had the great privilege of a medical centre, rare in those days. At that time it was very simple, with two wards, male and female, and one operating theatre, an out-patients and a fine dispensary. The original hospital is buried now within the extensions of the new buildings, but come, let me show you round." He beamed at Madeline. "I am really delighted to meet you, I have to say that this has really made my day." Madeline smiled warmly at him, trying to place his accent. Could it be Scottish Indian mix?

The original hospital, although certainly buried, was quite distinct, being built of thick stone walls, in handsome if severe lines. An arch opened into a courtyard in which a small fountain stood dry and surrounded with stone seats. Doctor Chandra showed them first the nurses' dormitory to the left which had been the female ward, then the theatre straight ahead which was now the lecture room. The male ward, to the right was now divided to provide accommodation for use of the young doctors. The ladies wandered around appreciating the coolness inside the thick-walled, high-ceilinged rooms.

"See!" the doctor pointed upwards. "We left the old, hand-pulled punkas. I am told that the rani insisted on installing them in case there was an electricity cut. Now they are of historical interest!" They gazed raptly at the early contraptions, ropes and pulleys which were the forebears of the electric fan.

"I am in awe, doctor," Madeline said. "I feel suddenly so close to my father who has been dead for many years. He did sometimes speak of it, of course. I believe he and the old maharani had a close bond, which in part must have been helped because Daddy wasn't a bad linguist." She turned a lovely smile on the doctor. "Thank goodness it wasn't demolished when the new buildings went up. And, doctor, thank you so much for showing us around. I cannot express my joy sufficiently. Had it not been for the old man, I might never have had the privilege of coming here."

A small commotion alerted them and the doctor frowned, obviously fearing some emergency. But it was Roger and the brigadier who hurried towards them, followed by the driver and the orderly.

"There you are Maddy!" He took her hand and gazed anxiously into her face. Reassured, he smiled and turned to the doctor and held out his hand. "Ah, Doctor Chandra, I see they are in good hands. The brigadier and I got some sort of garbled account about the two ladies, a snake and the old mali and of course we feared the worst. How is he?" he ended somewhat breathlessly.

Doctor Chandra bowed very slightly as he shook hands.

"Well, Highness, let us say that if the ladies had not brought the old one when they did, it might be another story. He'll mend. But really sir, will you use your influence to stop him from seeking out these generally harmless reptiles. It is his own fault, he provokes them, so of course they bite him. I have lost count of how many times he has been brought in. If you scold him, he may listen." They all smiled at this request.

Turning once again he shook hands with the brigadier standing in the shadows, led them out of the old courtyard and back into his office. More cold juice was brought, and the four visitors scrutinized the photographs on the walls.

Heads together, Roger and Madeline pointed out the young Doctor Muir to their new friends, till suddenly Roger said,

"Doctor Chandra, where is my grandmother?"

There was a startled silence, till understanding his gaffe, Roger laughingly re-phrased his question. "I should say, where is the statue, of my grandmother!?"

Up they got again and were led out through the sunlight, across courtyards to a corner of the compound where in a store-room, in the dimness, a young man was carefully chipping off layers of whitewash from the stone bust of a woman. They paused, while their eyes grew accustomed to the gloom.

"Ah, there you are grandmother!" Roger clapped his hands in delight and they stood about laughing at his enthusiasm. "She is actually sculpted from fine white marble, which merely needs a wash with lemon juice occasionally. But no, everything is whitewashed at least once a year, so she must be too." He leaned forward and prized off a chip. "Hundreds of layers I should say!"

"We heard that you were here, Highness," the doctor said remorsefully, "So I gave instructions that she be cleaned up. I am sorry, sir, that you see her undone. If you had come tomorrow she would have been back on her plinth in the entrance hall as usual."

"Splendid!" announced Roger very cheerfully. "We'll come back tomorrow to see the old man and grandmother, if that is OK with your doctor? But now, may we see him? Would it be possible? It might cheer him up."

The doctor led the way followed by Roger and Madeline with the Burroughs behind. Curious nurses, neat in white overalls, saris and white canvas shoes watched as the party approached the old patient. Leaning forward, it was obvious that Roger was speaking kind words to the old gardener who was all wired up to a drip and certainly did look very pale. Even so, he managed to smile and pressed his hands together in greeting.

A European woman approached them, and was warmly greeted by Doctor Chandra. She looked very smart all in white, a badge on her shoulder and wearing a blue belt with the familiar and beautiful silver buckle on it. Madeline took in the fair, slightly freckled skin and light red hair, and found herself somewhat astonished.

"Hello Matron," he turned to his guests. "May I introduce you to Matron, who also happens to be my wife, Fiona." They shook hands all round.

"How lovely to meet you," she particularly addressed Roger, then Madeline. "I heard that you were here, having brought in the old mali, but I was in the children's ward, always very time consuming, and could not get away. And," she beamed at Madeline, "to meet Doctor Muir's daughter! Such a privilege. He is still remembered as a great man in our little town."

Madeline listened and found herself hurriedly trying to sort out her startled impressions. Doctor Chandra's wife! The matron? Scottish!

"You are from Scotland?" she said, rather unnecessarily.

Both the director and his wife laughed. "I met her when I was a student and she was a trainee nurse," said the doctor. "She would not marry me, for very many reasons. Then, when her elderly parents died, at last she came out to visit me. We married, and," he raised his eyebrows in humour at his wife, "we hope to live here happily ever after."

Evening was falling, and the little party quietly sauntered out into the early dusk having given their thanks to the Chandras with promises to return on the morrow. A dog barked, a child cried, and the smell of wood-smoke and cooking filled the air. Then suddenly Roger asked, "Is there a chance, doctor, that you could join the team of old boys playing cricket against Saint Mathew's on Sunday? It will be a simple game, but I am urgently in need of two more chaps to make up our side."

The doctor looked a little startled, then obviously amused replied.

"Well sir, it is years since I played, but yes, for you, Highness, of course I will play. But be it on your head, for I am no longer very agile!"

"And how about asking my husband?" Mary Burroughs piped up, looking at the brigadier out of the corner of her eye. "He used to play for the army, and the county, and if you can provide him with a runner, for his leg won't run anywhere, I know he will be an asset to your team."

Surprised, delighted, they all grinned, shook hands again, while Roger quite beside himself with relief, made arrangements once more for the tailor to fit them up with whites, waving aside the blusters of the brigadier, and a rendezvous was agreed on at dawn the next morning for practice.

"All thanks to the old gardener too!" announced Madeline getting into the back of the car with the Burroughs. "My dear," she touched Mary Burroughs' hand, "thank you so much for your company and help. What a happy chance that you were on the veranda, I could not have managed without you."

"We'd like to invite you to dine with us," Roger called from the front seat as they drove back to the hotel. "We have some time to make up. Shall we meet on the dining room veranda at seven?"

Madeline waited for a reply, but accepted the silent nods and smiles as agreement. They must be so perplexed, she thought to herself. What with being my brother and being called "Highness", my Roger is quite an enigma to them. But, she settled more comfortably into the seat, it was good that they were friends now, and the cricket match would certainly be the highlight of their holiday.

CHAPTER FOURTEEN

THE MATCH

As usual the day dawned fair. Roger had been very abstemious over his meal the evening before, gone to bed early, and now, arrived bright and cheerful with their orange juices.

"Sit up, my love. Come on. Today's the day." He set her juice on her side table and drew a chair close to the bed. "Did you sleep well, Maddy mine? Will you be able to support your knight at the lists? Shall you be the most beautiful lady there?"

Madeline listened to his nonsense, thought about rolling over and going back to sleep but knew it wouldn't work.

"I am not yet ready to wake, you bully!" she said mildly, sitting up and accepting her glass of juice. Closing her eyes she sipped it. "I am going to miss all this luxury you know, back to reality next week, back to getting my own morning tea, breakfast, lunch and supper." She sighed deeply, willing the niggle of pain away from her stomach where it had lodged increasingly as the days fled past. "I am going to miss you, old dear. It has been a fabulous holiday, how I bless you for it."

Looking in the bathroom mirror she saw dark smudges under her eyes and frowned. At her age, what did she expect? So she decided that for once she would spend more than a little time on her face, just for Roger. Her best dress was hanging up, and she had managed to doll up her plain straw hat with a matching swathe of muslin, so she would look right. She had a really lazy day, resting in the cool of her veranda. The match was due to begin at four, so she must be ready to go with Mary to cheer on their men.

Word had apparently got around, for by the time they arrived at Saint Mathew's, there was a vast crowd edging the cricket pitch. The students, all in their best and fearfully handsome, were busily organizing everybody and showed Madeline and Mary Burroughs to their reserved seats under an awning against the sun.

It seemed that all the bigwigs of the town were there. Well, Madeline supposed, perhaps their sons were at the college, or maybe they themselves had been, or indeed were to play. She gazed about her fascinated. Lovely ladies smiled and nodded to her, their glorious saris bright, their jewels shining in the afternoon sunshine. Then, rather late, Fiona Chandra arrived breathless and a seat was found for her next to the English ladies. Of course she had been on the wards, she explained, for cricket or no cricket, people needed attention.

It started in a leisurely manner. The whites seemed dazzling in the sun, and Madeline felt sorry for the crowd on the other side of the pitch who had no shelter.

Gradually the scoring began, and the old boys strove to bowl, catch and run as the young boys. The brigadier was, true to his wife's word, a great cricketer. The doubtful silence which greeted his arrival soon changed to wild applause as his shots caused his young runner to dash for his life.

It could be anywhere, thought Madeline, the Home Counties, the South West, light clapping, the held breaths.

When Roger came on to bat, Madeline sat forward, clutching the edge of her seat. There was an awful moment when it looked as if he would be stumped, and Madeline quite forgot herself and yelled, "Roger!" to urge him on.

It was a moment, just a tiny moment of quiet in a noisy field, but her call was heard. For seconds there was silence, then as Roger flung himself into safety, suddenly the cry was taken up, "Raja, Raja, Raja!" The cry went on. It was all very exciting even if incorrect. For he was no longer a prince of India, he was just an old retired judge playing cricket for the fun of it. Yet here, in his birthplace, they knew him and to them he was still their prince. Madeline was secretly so delighted that he played well, and even if the college boys had manoeuvred a bare win, there had been some good playing.

When it was over, a great tea was spread in the hall of the college, the throng of invited guests, with no doubt some uninvited, milled about. Madeline was introduced to all the players of both sides, their wives, children and parents. Tea and refreshments were handed round by the college boys. It was a delightful if noisy affair with much good humour even at the children running underfoot.

Fiona Chandra brought her children to be introduced. Flora, the lovely eldest was very much in charge of two rascal boys who grinned shyly at the visitor and had to be threatened before they shook hands. Lastly, accompanied by their ayah, came enchanting twin girls who unlike their older brothers, were only too happy to be introduced. Glorious, limpid black eyes smiled sweetly at her.

Madeline could not hide her smile at their Scots accent. "They are so lovely and you dress them so beautifully, Fiona," Madeline said admiringly. Fiona smiled, then said quietly, "Their mother was really beautiful, and alas, of course being unmarried she could not care for twins, but as for the clothes." She laughed, "Ah, that I cannot take any credit for, that is all due to my aunt, who has made it her life's task to clothe not only our children, but to supply the children's ward. I am greatly indebted to her. But she loves doing it, for she scours all the jumble sales and charity shops, and every so often a veritable bale of clothes arrives, snail mail, of course."

"Has she ever visited you?" asked Madeline.

"Alas no," replied Fiona, "but perhaps when I tell her of your visit, it might give her courage to come."

Madeline thought for a moment.

"Would you like me to write to her on my return, Fiona, or phone, maybe I could persuade her as to how easy the journey is?"

"How kind of you, for I would really like the children to meet her, especially Flora who will be doing her training there before too long."

It was agreed that the ayah and the little girls would take an evening walk to the hotel with the address.

"They'll all love that," said the matron warmly.

"And perhaps I could give them tea?" asked Madeline with optimism.

"Even better dear lady, a huge treat. They will sleep well tonight." And bent to kiss her daughters roundly.

After they had gone their way to play outside with friends, Fiona said quietly to Madeline, "They are all our adopted children, Mrs. Eliot. By the time we married, I must have been rather past child bearing. So when one of my best nurses died in childbirth, we adopted Flora. The boys came along more or less by accident, being abandoned, and the twins, well, if it hadn't been for Flora's pleadings when they were abandoned by their mother in the nursery, I would not have taken them." She smiled happily.

"But now you see, we have a lovely family, and despite being so busy, my Flora is such a help, and with two ayahs, we manage."

Madeline liked Fiona Chandra and greatly admired her.

"Please call me Madeline, and tell me, do you ever come home? Will you come to visit me when you do? You might be interested to see our small nursing home too."

The other woman smiled gently and shook her head.

"Rarely, alas, although my husband does sometimes go on courses. We have such a busy, full life. We are needed in our little community, and we have our family. But yes, when I do come, I will surely let you know and perhaps?" She left a question in the air. "This is my home now, Mrs. Eliot, Madeline, and although I do have my aunt in Scotland with whom I am always in touch, there is little to hold me there. I expect to end my days here, and thankfully," she pulled a wry face, "it is not as hot here year round, as in other places. I don't believe I could cope in the South where I would frizzle up, so I consider myself very lucky."

Roger elbowed his way through the crowds to draw her out to the veranda where an elderly man sat in a fine, old basket wheel-chair. A fair skinned woman in European dress stood beside him.

"Madeline, meet old friends of mine, Mr. Mendoza, my grandmother's right hand and secretary and his daughter, Victoria, the heart throb of all the boys at Saint Mathew's in my day."

There were smiles and tongue clicking while Madeline shook their hands. The old man was so frail, his hand so cold, she held it in hers for a moment. He spoke in a whisper, so that his daughter had to lean down to catch his words before relaying them.

"Daddy says he is very, very glad to meet you Miss Madeline. He feels that he knows you, for he used to translate your letters to the rani, and they both enjoyed them so."

Madeline looked at each one, eyes round.

"My goodness, do you know I had forgotten all about those letters." She pressed the cold hands again. "They were because father insisted on Roger writing to his grandmother, so I did too, in way of support. And thank you for yours in return, I was so proud to show them to my school friends. A letter from Roger's granny who was a real queen in India! It gave me such kudos!"

The old man nodded smiling and went on whispering.

"He says," said his daughter, "she was also so pleased with the little sewing samplers you sent her, she kept them in her room all her life, and Daddy has them now."

Very slowly and carefully old Mr. Mendoza pushed aside the shawl which lay on his knees and tapped a small, very old red leather case. Looking up at Roger he strained to speak louder.

"Highness, your grandmother entrusted me with her last papers and I think the time has come for me to give them to you." His daughter carefully lifted the case and handed it to Roger. "Some you will have difficulty in reading, but I have done my best translating them, and should you need, there are some good scholars here who might help further."

Roger tucked the case under his arm, thanked him tenderly, pressing the cold hand.

Gradually the party dispersed while glancing at black clouds which filled the sky making it suddenly dark.

"Home, darling," Roger urged her, catching up with the Burroughs, to the car through milling crowds all eager for a handshake and farewells.

"We expect you to be our guests at dinner tonight," Roger pressed Fiona Chandra's hand. "No excuses now, the hospital will be there in the morning. Seven?" In the car he turned to the Burroughs, "And you too, if you will. Somehow it was such a very good day, I don't want it to end yet." They agreed whole-heartedly.

Back in their sitting room in the hotel, they went over the day, remembering little incidents, good shots, bungled catches and finally when their guests arrived, they all went to dinner together.

Tired, Roger quietly told them about the Mendozas.

"They are Portuguese Indians, from Goa, a fine people, who were in my family's service for years, I believe. My grandmother trusted old Mendoza as no one else. He knew many languages, was one hundred percent honest, the only flaw according to my grandmother was that he was a Christian and did not work on Sundays!" They laughed lightly, replete, tired, contented and conversation was easy.

Fiona told them a little about her home in Scotland, how she and her husband had met and a little of their protracted courtship.

"He allowed me to give the children Scottish names," she smiled lovingly at her husband. "Flora, the first, after my mother. Then Douglas, Duncan, Katrina and Kirsty. As the younger four were abandoned babies, we know little of their parentage, or indeed from what tribe or race they are from. But we do know that they are all very bright and who knows, they too

68

might do their training in Edinburgh as we did. That is their plan anyway." They smiled together.

"And are you really happy and settled here?" Mary Burroughs asked.

There was a small silence while Fiona thought. "There are times of course when I miss home. But I am indeed very happy, and since we have five children now, this is my home." She reached across to touch her husband's hand. "We are lucky, John and I."

A contented silence followed and Madeline looked at their new friends and was grateful too, because friends do make a holiday happier and more interesting.

After their guests had gone, Madeline and Roger pottered about in their sitting room. Roger glanced at the little case laid on the table. "I shall get stuck into that when you have left and I am home again twiddling my thumbs. I very much doubt there will be anything of interest in it, but it will be a good exercise for me and keep me busy. I was surprised and delighted to see old Mendoza again. Really it was a splendid day." He gently kissed Madeline. "Good night, dearest, sleep well."

It was with shock and sorrow that the very next day they were informed of Mr. Mendoza's death and were invited to attend his funeral the following day.

"It was such a relief to him that he had given you the rani's case, Highness." Victoria tried to hold back her tears. "He was insistent to see you, and he so much enjoyed his outing, and meeting you, Mrs. Eliot. His work with the rani was his life, you know. Her family was as his family, I am very grateful for his last day, and Highness, seeing you again. And that he went so quietly in his sleep, in his own bed." A small sob escaped her and Roger gently comforted her.

"At one hundred and one, Victoria, he did well. A most splendid old gentleman, I am proud to have known him and grateful for his years of service to my family." After the funeral which was held at a beautiful old Catholic church, they stayed with Victoria and her family till the last mourner had left.

The days were flying past and with the monsoons coming, Madeline and Roger made their farewells to old and new friends and sadly left the beautiful palace of Roger's youth.

I can't bear it, Madeline said to herself several times a day. I shall miss him so much. It will be dreadful being without him and alone again.

"Chin up chick," said Roger watching her, his heart aching too, "we have a few more days to whoop it up in Bombay. Come on, crack us a smile

Maddy." And Madeline tried, being quite unaware that he too was dreading her departure.

CHAPTER FIFTEEN

HOME AGAIN

"Thank you darling," she reached up to kiss her tall son. "I'll be fine. A good sleep is all I need." She walked into her little house, a glow of pleasure filling her and glad to see it very sick and span, no doubt just recently cleaned and polished for her arrival. A huge floral display dominated the fireplace.

"Oh, my dear, how very kind of you." Madeline turned to smile at her son who had put her cases down.

"Don't thank me, mother, Roger sent them, see," he touched a card tucked into the glorious bunch, "a note to welcome you. We have merely done the mundane things." He walked into the little kitchen and opened the fridge. "See, mother, all the basics you need, a quiche, salad, bread, butter, cheese, eggs and milk. We expect you for lunch day after tomorrow as usual. So I'll leave you now. Have a good sleep and don't hesitate to give us a buzz if you need absolutely anything, right?" He bent down to peck her cheek once.

"I'll bring all your gifts on Sunday shall I? By then I will have recovered and unpacked. Roger's family have sent you some beautiful things too so I'll come early. Will eleven do?" Madeline saw him to the door, waved, then shot the bolt and dropped the latch.

Tired, the sound of plane engines still in her head, she returned to the sitting room and looked at the flowers. They were lovely. So bright, so immensely cheerful, not at all what she felt. None the less she lifted the card and read the stranger's writing.

"Welcome to your little home, dearest Madeline," she smiled, hearing his voice in her mind. "I have asked for the gaudiest combination of colours they could find, to remind you of your hols. Catch up on your sleep. I'll be in touch soon. All love, R."

They had done well, she thought gazing at the splendid bouquet, mixing the most unlikely combination of colours which certainly did remind her of India. The bougainvillea, the glorious saris, the fruit and vegetables in the bazaar. Murmuring her thanks to the far distant Roge, she made herself a hot drink, then pottered about till at last she fell into bed.

The phone woke her and being for the moment quite disorientated, she fumbled for it, held it without speaking, trying to clear her mind.

"Maddy?" the voice was very dear and familiar. "Are you there, Madeline?"

"Oh yes, Roge," she tried to gather her wits. "Hello darling. How are you? Where are you?"

A chuckle came across the miles. "Oh dear, I woke you, didn't I? Oh I am so sorry love, I thought you'd be awake by now, I have been watching the clock for hours waiting for when you might have had enough sleep. Sorry!"

Madeline shook herself awake and glanced at the clock by her bed. Good heavens, eleven o'clock!

"So late!" she exclaimed, "I am the one to say sorry, half asleep here, unfit to speak coherently. But thank you, what a sleep. I will soon feel myself again when I have shrugged off the cobwebs."

There was a small silence, then they both began speaking together.

"I miss you so." Roger's voice was thick with emotion. "I just cannot believe that you are not here. It seems that you were always here, and now you have gone. How did I let you go? Why did I let you go? Maddy dearest, I miss you."

She held the phone so close to her ear it hurt but she didn't notice it really. He missed her! How wonderful, for she missed him too.

"Me too," she said softly, almost afraid of her feelings. "I thought it would never end, those wonderful three months, each day a joy. Yet it seems now that I took them for granted, and now I realize that I should have enjoyed them more. As I woke every morning I should have marked it as very special and not just have meandered away the time. I thank you for all you did for me, and your dear, charming family, who made me so welcome. No one could have been more blessed than I was during that beautiful holiday."

"So you will come again?" he sounded as a small boy, beseeching. She laughed.

"Try to stop me! But of course I will. I shall start saving up immediately, maybe I will let the lodge next autumn as our friend the agent suggested. Then I could come for six months and we could travel around. I could put my belongings in the roof, now it is properly lined, my treasures at the big house. But next time I come Roge, I insist on paying my way, because now you are retired, and whatever you say, a guest costs. So on that basis, please may I come again next year?"

A warm chuckle was followed by assurances that anything she wanted, he would agree with, so long as she promised she would come.

"I'll call again tonight," he said now quite cheerfully. "I feel much happier now that I know you are safely home again. So dear one, till then, rest, take it easy, blessings on your head."

She did. Happy now with the warmth of his voice, his blessing, she went about the little house still in a daze but slowly achieving some order. Her two cases were open and gradually emptying. The pile of gifts grew on the sofa, her clothes on a chair, a few pieces of laundry on the floor. There was no hurry of course, no train or plane to catch, no rendezvous. Then she suddenly realized that she hadn't thanked him for the flowers and felt wretched, thought to phone, but restrained herself. It could wait. He'd understand and she'd thank him when he rang later. Then she might be more awake and able to describe their glorious and wild colours.

The days passed slowly and Madeline gradually resumed her old regime while sleeping in the afternoon, a habit she decided she'd keep, and writing up her diary and letters in the evening, instead of going to bed early.

Roger rang regularly. Their conversations were warm and loving and Madeline wondered at how she ran to the phone, how her breath would come a little short, and how her heart would beat a little faster.

"You are behaving like a girl in love!" she admonished herself.

"Don't be silly," the sensible pensioner, Madeline, replied. "Roger is your brother. You love him as you always did, as family."

The photographs were ready and she asked her son to send them to India by E-mail so that they would get there quickly.

"I wish I could learn to use that thing, it is so clever, so quick, not like hand-writing," she told her older grandson, who promptly offered to teach her. But Madeline declined, convinced she could never learn.

Whenever she went to the village, Madeline made a point of looking up their old school friends to tell them of her trip and show them the photographs. Despite the years, there were many still in the district. It was lovely how, all those years ago at the church school, all their mates had totally accepted Roger, despite his being different. For in the wilds of the West Country, there were few foreigners just after the war, let alone any with brown skins.

She remembered a time when they had all been lying on the green, the girls making daisy chains.

"There!" had said Madeline, carefully placing her crown on Roger's shining black hair. "King Roger of England!" They had all rolled about laughing, revelling in the warm day and lack of school.

"He can't be king of England, Maddy!" said Jessy Quin, "he isn't even English!"

A cloud crossed the path of the sun and for a moment it was cold.

"Ah," announced Roger standing up, one hand on a hip, the other raised in salutation, "that is where you are wrong. I am a prince of England inside, with a brown skin outside. BUT!" He raised his finger in mock repetition of a frequent saying of their headmaster, "It is what is inside which matters!" And they laughed again, but kindly. Madeline never forgot that day.

"You'll have to get him to come and stay here for a while," said Jim Woolacott, leaning over the fence of his cottage. "We can have a reunion, for I see that everyone seems to be doing it nowadays. After all, almost fifty odd years is a good stretch."

Madeline happily agreed and they planned on passing on the word to see if it was feasible.

Spring had come, early as it always did in the West Country and in sheltered places the flowers were out and when they spoke on the phone, Madeline told Roger about them, where she'd found them and that she had picked some white and deep mauve violets, just for him.

As time went on, she felt that they had become closer, because over the phone there was just the two of them. No one else was around. No meetings to go to, no demands, just precious moments of speaking. She recognised that probably she was in love with him, as well as loving, indeed as well as liking him. How odd. How very peculiar after all those years, to find that she loved Roger. As a man, as even a lover, at their age? And what would people say? Her family? Her friends? The village? They'd laugh, and yes, no doubt they'd disapprove, being conservative in their thinking about different races intermarrying. My goodness, she thought, now you think the word marriage, Madeline, pull yourself together, grow up. It had seemed so far-fetched and ridiculous when it first had hit her. Yet now she accepted it, and marvelled that she, in her sixties could feel the sheer glory of loving. Of course no one would ever know. Certainly not!

This, she would keep safely in her heart, a most precious secret. And it was hers, this great and beautiful love, hers alone, and no one, but no one, could take it away. Having accepted how she felt, she became happier and lighter having dismissed her surprise and doubts. Yet now and again she would find herself smiling quietly, marvelling with the joy of her new-found love.

CHAPTER SIXTEEN

THE RED CASE

Roger sat on his veranda, a tray of tea on the table beside him untouched, the photocopies in his hands. What a splendid holiday it had been. He could not understand why they hadn't done it before. Ridiculous to have left it so long. He reached for his tea and sighed. He did not, he had begun to realize, feel very well. There was a strange ache in his gut although he had eaten very sparingly of late. Perhaps, as his daughter told him, despite the joy, it had been too much. It seemed so lonely now, whereas before Maddy had come out, he had revelled in his privacy. Of course there was no job to keep him busy any more. That would be it. He had heard of people dropping dead six months after they retired! Well, he wouldn't, he had far too much to do. Even so, if the pain in his gut did not go away soon, he would have to go to see the doctor.

After he had finished his tea, he reached for the red leather case which dear old Mendoza had given him. Here now was a project, sorting out all the ancient, fusty papers which his grandmother had so carefully preserved and entrusted to her secretary. There must be something of interest in there, he opened the lid and peered in. Faint mixed scents of rose, of incense, jasmine, of musty old paper and leather, they were echoes of the past. But surely they reminded him of her, she who had been so steadfast and wise and she who had truly loved him. The trouble was where to begin. He gazed incredulously at the funny little yellowing pieces of cloth, apparently painstakingly sewn by Maddy and sent to his grandmother, and smiled broadly, he must tell her about them.

He called for the butler who immediately appeared and together they set up another table on which they set several paper-weights.

As night fell and the mosquitoes came out, the tables were carefully carried in and Roger continued his investigation, fascinated. He wished he had a secretary there to write down what he read. But then he realized that many of the papers were so personal, she had meant them for him alone. Or rather, Mr. Mendoza and him. For the writing was mostly in Mendoza's fine hand, although in places the ink was very faded.

It was a relief having something to do, and something to talk about instead of moping. Certainly he did feel better, and he realized that although he still missed Maddy, the empty feeling was less, because in his mind he was sharing his thoughts with her, while deep into the contents of the old red case.

That evening Madeline phoned him, it being Sunday and a low price call, so he was able to tell her his findings. Each subject was carefully wrapped in strong brown paper as an envelope and tied with red ribbon, similar to legal papers. Some of the contents were just fragments of paper, so thin, he handled them very carefully. Some were receipts for cloth, silver, jewels while others were more mundane, menus for, looking at the quantities, he pulled a face, apparently vast banquets. So slowly, one by one he was going through them. First of all rather roughly to asses their contents, then later, he would go over them more carefully. Up till now it seemed mostly family history, which he would hand to his son after making copies for the girls.

On the third packet, he found himself fascinated by accounts of great tamashas. Which maharajas attended, and how many elephants they had brought. What great British gentlemen came, with their wives and entourage. Her opinions in her own hand were written in the side margins, very small, some, quite humorous.

"Oh Roge!" Madeline exclaimed. "If you could get that nice old man who did your father's diaries to translate them into English for me, maybe we could publish a small book together?"

They were excited by the thought, so Roger located his old clerk, who was now living in his old home out of the city. Fortunately he was only too pleased to take on a little job to wile away his empty, retired days. Not only would it give his still fine brain work to do, it would bring in some welcome money. But above all, the old clerk smiled in his sleep in anticipation, it would give him kudos in the village. With the windows and doors wide open during the day, the gentle tapping of his old typewriter could be heard by everyone who passed by. There lived a learned man!

Then, Roger did not phone for several days, and Madeline was anxious as only the butler answered when she called saying that the sahib was away.

At last he called.

"Maddy, Maddy dearest, I am North again, I had to come on business about something, hence I didn't phone. No, that is not why I didn't phone. I have something exciting and private to relate. Maddy! I need to speak to you."

Madeline listened, a small frown between her eyes.

"Roger! I am here dear one. Are you ill? What-ever is the matter, you sound so odd?" There was a pause. Then more urgently she repeated, "Roger, are you alright?"

After another pause she heard him, but far away, probably because there was a storm coming up and the line was poor.

"How would you like me to come to stay with you?" A cry of joy reached him very clearly. "Ah, good," he cut in before she could reply. "You would like me to come!"

They laughed happily and suddenly Madeline felt flustered and realized that her hair needed a trim and her nails had suffered gravely from her morning's weeding. "I'll ring when I have done the booking and I'll come directly, OK?"

Now he felt full of life and brimming with excitement. There was so much to tell, so much to explain. But how could he? It was really so very complicated.

When almost to the bottom of the red case, he had begun to feel that something very strange was about to reveal itself. Firstly, he had opened the sheets on which were several horoscopes, beautifully drawn. His grandmother had intensely believed in such matters and had a trusted old astrologer who guided her every move, or so it had seemed. There, beautifully drawn was her own horoscope and unbelievably, Doctor Muir's! Gracious! Then, there were other horoscopes, his, his late wife Lella's, and the three children's. And lastly, there was Madeline's. Madeline and dad's horoscope! He gazed at them shocked. For goodness sake, why ever had she had them done? He gazed at first one then the other, front and back, read and re-read what he could make of it, but was none the wiser. Puzzled, he re-wrapped them and put them back in the case to bring out the last envelope.

If he had been surprised by the horoscopes, now he was amazed by the contents of this last package. It was full of drawings. Furniture? Carvings! He leafed through the sheets, frowning incredulously. Every detail of a small carved chest was there, perfectly executed on paper as they were on the real thing, the wood.

There were accurate drawings of scissors and button hooks, needles, bobbins and thimbles. There were the neatest sketches of hinges and a lock. And beside them very lightly was written the weight and the cost of the gold.

Then, his breath coming fast, he began to understand. He recognized every little perfect drawing there. Life-sized as it were, they were as familiar to him as were his shoes, his fountain pen. Hadn't he watched Maddy using it lovingly for years and years. It was her work box, the only large gift which had been accepted, despite his grandmother's persistent pleas. There on the lid were Maddy's initials.

With his hands trembling, Roger went on, page after page, gazing in disbelief at the exquisite drawings, as photographs, of Madeline's little work chest.

Cross sections of the legs, hollow? Even the weight and cost of pure bees wax plugs was carefully written. He put the sheets down and rubbed his eyes. This wasn't real! Inside the hollow legs were drawn twists of cloth, and four lines wrote of gems, one for each leg. Diamonds, rubies, sapphires and emeralds. Their respective quantities, their weight and cost. Grief, he thought, a veritable treasure-chest.

His mind flew back over the years to his grandmother cussedly insisting that he took the chest by plane as a special gift for Madeline. It was to be for her dowry, she said, a girl needed a beautiful work box to encourage her to sew. On and on she went, insisting that it accompany him, lavishly packed up and totally disregarding the cost of flying it, causing him to be grossly overweight.

So dear grandmother, he said in his mind, you crafty old woman. You knew that one day I would love Maddy, and you did not accept that she would come to me without a dowry. Amazing! And all these years it has sat beside her chair, a much loved and very much used piece of furniture. Oh my goodness, he shook his head in wonderment, most wise and excellent grandmother.

Roger sat back in his chair and mused over his astonishing discovery. Had old Mendoza known of it? He must have, probably the only one alive to do so apart from the carpenter and the jeweller. When had she done Madeline's horoscope? He searched in his mind, sought through the papers and yes, there it was, the date but more, the name of the astrologer. Then his mind quickened. Such work was usually passed from father to son. He wondered if any of the astrologer's family still lived and worked. He would find out, and he would go North once more if briefly, for he must learn all he could about these charts.

Had she known he would end up by loving Maddy? Had she planned everything? Why? Thoughts flew through his mind and unconsciously he shook his head as if it were all too much. Had she loved Dad? Of course not, she was much older than he. But was she? For he knew that she had married at thirteen. Yes! It was as if a bright shower of stars fell. She had loved him, the gentle English doctor who chance had brought to her door. Another revelation swept into his brain, that is why she built the hospital, to keep him discreetly with her, for as long as she could.

Roger put his head in his hands. Oh the poor darling! With her empty life of luxury, which despite being the rajas wife, she had shared with her raja's endless other women. The boredom of her days, the lack of any mental stimulation which was her lot. Was it so very odd that her eye and heart had lighted on the handsome, young foreigner and she had loved him? He who had nursed him when he was so ill, then her. Tears filled his eyes. Oh grandmother, a silent cry rose from his throat, did you want me to know? Is that why you sent me to England, to be with your beloved, to ease your longing, your loss, your pain?

"Oh, my God," Roger spoke aloud. "Now I understand!"

CHAPTER SEVENTEEN

UNRAVELLING THE COBWEBS

In the end she went to the station herself and waited in the bright spring sunshine, fearful with anticipation. First Jim had said he would go. Then she thought of ordering the village taxi. At last she thought the best thing would be to meet him, impersonally, with lots of people around so that she wouldn't make a fool of herself.

Having changed several times, she ended by up looking very casual, which was how he always liked her. If he was very tired, she'd call a taxi, if not, they could take the bus which went in fifteen minutes from outside the station. She fiddled in her pocket with her door keys. Perhaps when she saw him again she would regain her sanity. Her heart seemed to flutter, and she felt like a girl waiting for her boy. Above all, she must not embarrass him. That would not do. So play it cool she would, and at least they had something new to speak about, the putting together of the book, and the proposed school reunion.

It worked beautifully. With his usual gusto he hugged and kissed her and insisted that they wait for the bus in the tea room opposite. It helped that Maggie Phelps ran it, for although younger than both of them, they had known her most her life and she was full of enthusiasm for the school reunion.

"By this time tomorrow," Roger said happily, linking his arm in Madeline's as they stood at the bus stop, "the whole town will know that I'm home."

Roger hadn't seen the refurbished lodge so she showed him round proudly and basked in his real delight and praise.

"What a clever thing you are," he hugged her lightly, "who could imagine that this tiny, very dull little lodge could turn out so charming and practical."

They had tea in the conservatory which overlooked the lawns towards the big house. Their conversation was easy, if just a little less cheerful than when they were together in India. Madeline felt that she was gabbling. Roger thought that he wasn't contributing to the conversation as usual and put it down to being tired. He yawned.

"How thoughtless of me, of course, dearest. You are tired! How could I be so careless, come, let me show you to your little room. A good sleep is what you need and we will both be happier tomorrow."

But they weren't. A curious cloud seemed to sit over their heads. Conversation was stilted, even talk of the book was half-hearted. Madeline looked sadly out of the kitchen window, the pain in her heart almost unbearable. What had happened to them? Where was the joy, the love, affection and laughter they had always shared. A tear fell into the washing-up water and she crossly brushed it away with a soapy hand.

"Here," Roger was by her side, "let me." Very tenderly he wiped the tears and pulled her close. Which only made it worse, for Madeline then let go of her pent up emotions and just wept. When she had stopped, without a word he continued mopping her eyes, and as with a child, held his hanky to her nose to blow. She giggled. He held her tighter.

"I love you Maddy," he spoke into her hair, throwing caution to the winds. "Yes I know I am an old man with little to offer, but I love you with my life. Yes as a sister and a friend, but as a woman too, a lovely, good, sweet woman. Don't laugh at me, Maddy mine. It came so slowly while you were staying with me, that I didn't believe it possible. I don't remember a more happy time in my adult life. Then when you left I felt ill, yes, really ill, without you. I just wanted to be with you and I must be truthful, it was why I thought up the book, any excuse to be with you again." He kissed her hair and revelled in the sweet fresh smell of it. "Are you angry with me? Will you tell me what a damned old fool I am and send me away? Have I embarrassed you horribly?"

Madeline leaned into him and smiled wetly, dabbing at his clean shirt. Imagine, he felt the same as she did, and they hadn't known. Slowly she raised her head and smiled at him.

"We always did think the same, didn't we?"

His eyes opened very wide above her, a query in them. She just gave the slightest nod and without warning, he whirled her off the ground and around twice before putting her down, then held her tightly again.

"Enough of that, you hoodlum," she mock-scowled at him, breathless. So he just bent his head and kissed her very tenderly first on each cheek, then her forehead, her chin and then, unbelievably sweetly, on her mouth.

They somehow got to the sofa and sat close holding both hands. They talked, they laughed, Madeline shed a few more tears. They discussed their feelings as lovers do when they first are aware of their love.

"Roge, most dear, I love you!" She had to say it, loud and clear. "I just could not believe it, I thought that I was an old fool," she emphasised the I. "I was afraid that if you found out, you would be cross, would laugh at me, so I hid it."

"Come!" he demanded, "sit on my lap, you foolish old dame," and hauled her on his lap. Grateful, she leant into him. "Everything that you have just said, I know about, because all those thoughts were chasing around my head too. Darling, I love you so, though I could never believe that an old fellow like me could feel this way."

They sat quietly, listening to each other's breathing, the bird-song outside, the distant hooter of the quarry. Then Roger settled her, got up and drew up a stool, sat on it facing her.

"Another terrible doubt I have to explain to you, slowly and carefully, to make sure that you don't misconstrue my words."

He opened the red box. Some of its contents she had heard over the phone but he pressed her hand, absently tidied a stray lock of hair which fell on her brow. It must be told carefully and in order. He began with how he had gone north to track down the astrologer who his grandmother had used and found his grandson.

"This was something so personal, I felt only I could do it and did not want to entrust the task to anyone else. I was so lucky to find him, that his family had survived and that he had inherited his father's and grandfather's business. He is an intelligent, well educated young man, with all the knowledge and wisdom of his forebears. I explained my surprise at finding that my grandmother had not only done many family horoscopes, she had included your father's and yours. It was perplexing, why should she do them also? I asked the astrologer to look particularly at yours and mine, and to examine them in order to understand her actions. I spent that night with my old friend Dee, who you met. I couldn't face the palace and the memories. Next day I returned to the astrologer and spent an hour with him. He explained everything to me. It was fascinating." A great sigh escaped him.

"Maddy, my darling, I hope this won't shock you, for it was quite a revelation to me. My grandmother loved your father. Of this I am now quite certain. That is why she asked for him to stay to help build and set up the hospital. Oh I am sure it was a most pure and innocent love, and only on her part. For dad was younger, and so serious, he surely can't have had any inkling of her true feelings? She was a very quiet, traditional woman who knew her place, and don't forget, adultery by Indian women was certainly, at that time, a very serious offence. It would have ruined him too, and she thought far too much of him for that." He paused, kissed her softly and continued. "That is why she sent me to you, it wasn't only for my leg. The contact. To have me, who she loved totally, to be with the only man she had ever loved. The astrologer showed me the signs on both their charts. There were many similarities, but clearly, a great yet unfulfilled love. Which was, I assume, sublimated in the organizing and building of the hospital, giving her an intense interest for the rest of her life. Not that I understood much of the charts, they seem so complicated, but certainly I saw the similarities he spoke of in them. I'll show you them all afterwards."

Roger sighed deeply again and it was Madeline's turn to caress him.

"Why the sigh love? Aren't we together now. There is no need to sigh so."

For a moment he held her close, easing back on the sofa, arm thrown about her shoulders, he stared out of the window at the evening.

"That is not all, Maddy. There is more, and I don't know quite how to tell you. It seems that I have got this whole business round the wrong way, whichever way I approach it."

She looked at him fondly. Such a dear, familiar face. "Just get on with it, love. Share it with me. You know me well enough by now to know I won't react badly, however way you tell it."

Grateful, he hugged her again. "I would like to stay with you all the remaining years of my life. There you see, back to front. What I should have said was, I'd like you to stay with me for the rest of our lives." They laughed lightly and felt very close.

"Go on."

"After you left, when I felt so down, I was aware that you were the source of my happiness, and my unhappiness. Perhaps a relationship between us as man and woman, might be considered incestuous. Yet," he pressed a firm kiss on her brow, "we are not in fact in any way related.

Neither are we in our first youth, understatement, but, and forgive me again if what I say is out of place, I do desire you, Maddy mine."

There was a silence, but unable to reply, Madeline pressed into his side to show him that his words were not unwelcome.

"I would like to make you my wife. I would love, you to be my wife. How many ways can I find to tell you that?" She smiled broadly but she still didn't answer. "Then," he sighed deeply yet again, "we are from such different backgrounds. I am Indian and I have a brown skin, even if I think and speak as an Englishman. You are English and you have," he hesitated and lifted her hand to his lips, "a pale, pink skin." She made to speak but he hushed her. "Let me finish, darling, please. You saw how the Burroughs disapproved of your being with me at the palace? How when they learned of our innocent relationship, they thawed. Oh yes I know that things are aeons more relaxed now than they were when dad and my grandmother were young. But even so, I couldn't bear to have what I feel for you result in any unpleasantness for you."

Now Madeline firmly spoke up.

"Yes you are Indian, and as dad said, possibly part Persian, even part Greek, from way back. You could be Spanish, or Italian, or Greek. You are British too, or had you forgotten? Your skin is a lovely soft, pale café-au-lait, and your eyes are an interesting North Sea grey," she laughed, "gosh, that rhymes! But I am serious. Is there any need for anyone to know if we marry or not. You are YOU. Very special, deeply loved for many years by me and my family. Indeed accepted, loved and respected by the village and townsfolk. Your skin colour has never been anything to us, which well you know." She paused and touched his face tenderly. "We can still be together, six months here and six months there, or whatever. Both our families accept us as adopted siblings. All my friends, our friends and your friends have always been most loving towards both of us. Ours is an interesting story. Is there any reason to change it?

Roger stared at her hard.

"You mean to live together, as brother and sister, share our homes and our countries, so be together?"

Madeline felt a twinge of unease, for she had never been a bold woman. It wasn't what she meant at all. "Did I understand you a moment ago? Were you proposing marriage to me or not?" She looked him in the eye.

"I was asking you to marry me!"

"Then!"

"Then what?

"Roger, what I am saying is, why should we not marry privately, quietly, and no one need know. We can live together for evermore to the outside world as siblings. Just we, you and I, will know that we are also husband and wife and be happy."

"We'll need one more person, a witness."

"We will find that person!"

"Well how about that then?" said Roger, grinning, suddenly feeling brighter. "Nothing is insurmountable if you want it enough. Remember dad saying that?"

They grinned at and reached for each other.

"You are right as he was, nothing is insurmountable, and I want you very much. Will you marry me then, Madeline?"

"I will, Raja!"

CHAPTER EIGHTEEN

MADELINE'S DOWRY

"There is more, my love. Again I have put it the wrong way round." Roger shook his head and his fine silver hair flopped into his eyes. Madeline brushed it back tenderly. "I felt that first I wanted to tell you of my love, to ask you to marry me. But now I have to tell you something pretty important. It might have changed your decision. You might think that I am after your fortune."

Madeline stared at him, then burst out laughing. "What fortune, Cuckoo? You know that I have handed over my share of the manor to Jim for tax reasons, and that I have this lodge for my lifetime, and receive a modest sum monthly from the nursing home he runs, as well as my pension. Anyway, if I did have a fortune I'd share it with you, as well you know."

"Your dowry, Maddy," Roger continued, as if he hadn't heard her. "The dowry which my grandmother provided for you, through her love of dad and, having learned from me that dowries don't exist here. Also, she did it for you believing her astrologer's forecast of our later lives together and probably also to keep herself busy." He got up, kissed her lightly and went to his room to return immediately carrying the red case. "It is time now to show you everything, and to explain to you what I believe and hope will be, your dowry."

They sat close with the case on Roger's knee. Madeline watched as he carefully went through the papers in their wrappers till at the bottom, he drew out the one with the drawings of the work box in.

"My work box!" Madeline said, surprised.

"Yes, your work box Maddy, and your dowry, darling. Yes, it is almost unbelievable, see, just see what she planned." He held up the sheet of paper with the drawings of the implements, hinges and escutcheon, "As we suspected, they are gold, not brass, because they never needed cleaning." They peered closely and Roger translated the beautiful oriental writing on the side. "Now I realize that all this was really done for love of your father. How dad would laugh, for I don't suppose he guessed anything of her emotions." He drew out the next sheet. "See, my love, here is your little sewing chest, every detail, built in teak, which is why it is so heavy. We always wondered at its dumpy design. Well now we know. And, look here, these are the drawings of its inner secret, the cross sectioned legs. They are hollow."

Madeline looked at the drawings, then at Roger.

"Golly!" she said, still unknowing.

"And now," he pointed to the fine writing, "look here, details of what are hidden in the legs."

Madeline's eyes grew rounder. His finger traced the list carefully and read. "Diamonds, rubies, sapphires and emeralds. One lot in each leg." They sat silently, gazing at, perhaps not seeing, the neat list. "You are a wealthy woman, Maddy, how wealthy I do not know, for undoubtedly these are old stones and would need re-cutting. However, they must surely be of the finest quality, for understanding the great care my grandmother took over this project of hers, I suspect, you have here the best of everything." More silence, but close, close.

"I wish I had met her."

"Yes, she'd have liked that, particularly as she believed that you would eventually be my bride!"

Madeline turned and laughed at him,

"Really! But, doesn't that sound lovely?"

"Each time when I went back, armed with photographs, I had to tell her all about you. And of course she loved those funny little school samplers you made her, and even if she couldn't read them, she treasured your quaint letters." He paused again, deep in thought. "Now, only now with all these revelations do I finally understand what motivated her. The great love she had for a good man. Amazing, and in some ways, very sad. Yet, quite obviously, it gave her happiness, it must have, because in her own way, she managed things very well. Not forgetting, that her secret project in supplying you with your dowry, kept her busy. And all the while she must have had some quiet satisfaction in doing it behind everyone's back."

They sat very quietly for a while, Roger remembering his loving but very firm grandmother, Madeline just wondering at the unusual and touching story.

Suddenly she jumped up and pulled at his hand.

"Come along darling, let's go for a walk, for I heard the forecast that it will rain tomorrow."

They walked peacefully, hand in hand all around the lanes about the Manor, often gazing down to the little town and far out to sea. Occasionally Roger would drop a kiss on her brow, or her cheek or her lips. Gently, sweetly, to show his love for her without causing her any alarm.

At the church Madeline took the great key from its hiding place and they went in quietly. To her mild surprise Roger took her by the hand and led her up the aisle till they stood before the altar. Then, he knelt, and Madeline followed.

"Before God, I take thee Madeline, for my wife," and looked intently her.

Then a wide-eyed Madeline, quickly replied,

"Before God, I take thee Roger, for my husband." They stayed there silently with their own thoughts for a few moments, and then he helped her rise.

"Come, let us go out to the grave to tell mother and dad." Hand in hand they walked through the ancient tombstones, the grass springy under their feet. Then they stood silently before the headstone of Madeline's parents, and Roger's foster parents, and both spoke with their minds of their happiness, their gratitude.

Madeline felt a great lump in her throat and she blinked hard. The past moments had been so unexpected, beautiful and natural. If only life could really be so simple.

They slowly returned by the big house, enjoying the setting sun and the lovely views. There they had a sherry with the family where as usual, Roger was made warmly welcome and talk was light and general. The nursing home was doing well. There were several permanent patients, and a few in for respite. Jim's wife Caroline had been a nurse, so they ran it together in a very professional way. Yet, having been his home, Jim treated his patients as guests, so the atmosphere was altogether very relaxed. He took Roger around, showing him all the improvements, large and small. The huge new conservatory, where the patients spent most of their time, the lift, and the small surgery, where he also had his practice. It had worked out well and Roger did not feel the sadness he half expected in seeing his childhood home changed so much. They talked too about The Book, which Roger claimed was his reason for coming. The family were excited about it, and demanded to be the first to read it.

After waving to them from the French windows, Jim said absently to his wife.

"If I didn't know those two, I'd have said that they are in love."

Caroline Eliot paused, leaning against the doorframe as her husband retreated into the room. So she saw Roger lift her mother-in-law's hand to his lips. Pleased, she smiled privately to herself. Men! They didn't really understand a thing.

That night Madeline and Roger drew the curtains after their light supper and sat at the kitchen table on which the sewing box stood waiting to reveal its secrets.

"There is mention of beeswax here," he pointed to the item in the list. "We must empty it I'm afraid, Maddy, for I suspect that the way into the legs is from the top, from inside the chest."

Maddy took out the top tray which held all the practical implements and laid it on the table. Fetching her largest tray and a roasting tin she scooped out her years of bits and pieces till the chest was empty. Then she gave it a quick wipe with a damp cloth and they both peered in.

"There must be a false bottom, Maddy, for I don't see any circles of wax, or indeed any fixtures for the legs in the corners." He examined it carefully. "A hook might be the answer?"

Madeline quickly went to the top tray she had just taken out and produced two beautiful gold crochet hooks, one larger than the other.

"I see two small indentations in the floor, look," he pointed and Madeline peered in too. "If we insert the two hooks, juggle them up and down a little, the base might loosen and come up. Let us try." They did and at first, dust and age caused it to stay firm but then it began to move. Very gently they lifted up the edge of the thin slice of wood which made the false bottom. To their satisfaction, up it came revealing a dusty floor underneath. Madeline once again gave it a good wipe around and there, clear to see, were wax roundels in the corners.

"Now," Roger felt them with his fingers, "they are so hard, I think we must use heat to melt them a little." It was a slow job, with various efforts using hot water, then the iron, till Madeline announced that they should just open one corner, the others could wait.

"You are right darling, and this is yours. You choose which corner you want to open and by now the wax must be just a little soft, we'll chip it off with a knife."

Madeline chose the corner closest to her, the front, right hand one, and Roger carefully prized off the wax disk revealing a hole.

"Take up the crochet hook again, Maddy, go on, you fish about in there and see what you can find."

It was a great moment, and they looked at each other, eyes alight, like children. Carefully at first, Madeline poked the hook in, but came up with nothing, then more daring she delved in deeper, and the hook caught. Very gently she drew it up and a twist of deep pink silk slid out. Laying it on the table, she first gazed at it and then at him.

"Well, go on darling. It is yours to do with what you want. On second thoughts wait, perhaps a dish or bowl might be a good idea."

So Madeline took a small glass bowl out of a cupboard and set it on the table. Carefully she pulled at the threads which held the silk roll together. Then again she quickly searched for her familiar golden scissors, snipped at the thread and unrolled it. At last, as a frozen cascade, myriad stars of intense light trickled from the silk into the bowl, their brilliance shining up at them. They sat silently as the stones fell gently with a sweet tinkling sound into the glass bowl.

"Diamonds!" said Roger.

"Golly!" said Madeline. She put her finger into the little ice cold heap of stones and pushed them around wondering at the brilliance of them.

"Look," Roger said, "some are cut and others are rough, alluvial."

A flash of blue caught her eye.

"Oh look, Roge, a blue one. Do you suppose it is a sapphire which got in there by mistake, or is it also a diamond?" They pondered on the beautiful blue pebble.

"I am pretty sure it is a diamond, not that I know anything about them, but she was so thorough. I did read somewhere that coloured diamonds do exist and that they are rare. But only recently are they in demand, therefore very precious. But we shall have to find out." He paused and frowning, went on. "Now I remember that stone. She wore it always in a little traced basket of gold. It was her most loved piece, and I think I remember she told me that it had been her mother's".

"But how will you dispose of them? Who on earth can we ask, indeed trust? This, my darling is quite a tricky business. If you want to sell them as I am sure you do, we must find a most reliable jeweller."

They looked at each other, slightly crestfallen. Then Madeline jumped up and went to her room. When she returned she had two small boxes in her hands.

"These pieces were Mummy's," she said. "I vaguely remember daddy giving them to her for a special birthday or anniversary. She thought a lot of these two pieces and loved them as I do." She peered at the inside lid where on white satin a name was written. "Karrendski," she read. "Yes, I remember now. Mummy told me that there was a patient staying when the house was a military nursing home. I remember the name Karrendski as it was unusual, and he stayed with us for a while. I'm sure that his family had a clock and jeweller's shop in London, maybe they still exist?"

Roger went to the phone and rang enquiries while Madeline carefully rolled up the stones in the silk again and putting them on the floor of the chest, shut and locked it.

The next day they phoned Karrendski's, who sure enough did still exist and Madeline asked for their address. Then she sat down and wrote, asking if someone could come to see them on a private matter.

"I think it would be the best way, darling," Roger had said, beginning to feel nervous about the whole operation. "It seems that Karrendski's is still a family firm and it could be that your old patient may still be alive. It might be best to find out what sort of people they are before showing them the whole lot. In fact we must not reveal anything of their provenance or tell them about the other legs and their contents. If you just show him one or two stones, it would make a start."

Madeline looked at him, eyes shining with love.

"Roge dearest, do you see what this means? We can be truly married and live together without any financial worries. We can travel with ease and comfort. We can help the children, the hospital." Her eyes lighted up again. "I'd like to invite Victoria Mendoza to stay, let us say for a month, we'll pay for everything, of course. One week here, then the three of us can go to Portugal together for two weeks, to fulfil her life's dream. Then a fourth week here! Oh Roger darling, what an amazing, clever woman your grandmother was. Her secret gift will benefit not only us, but so many people. Oh Roge, are we not really, very much blessed."

He held her close, tight, kissed her tenderly, hard, sweetly, fiercely, every way he could, smothering her head, neck and shoulders with love.

"So we will get properly married, my darling girl, sister, friend, love of my life. And then, quietly and securely, God willing, for the rest of our allotted time, we can live happily ever after!"

CHAPTER NINETEEN

THE BROTHERS

Algie had visited again. Together, almost with hesitation despite their anticipation and excitement, they gently they came out with the story and finally, Algie held his breath when they opened up the little work box and showed him the bowl of diamonds.

"I am speechless my friends. This is really something big. Too big for me or my nephew, Tim. What I really I wish is that my elder brothers were here to advise, they are far more knowledgeable than I am on gems, know the market better with their larger shops in the States and France. Their sons are real experts too. Do you think? May I ask you a huge favour? I would like to invite them to come over to experience the opening, the sheer excitement and joy of discovery. May I?"

Both Roger and Madeleine laughed and both spoke at once, interrupting each other with their enthusiasm.

"Of course, of course, wonderful, invite them to come."

Fortunately, most of the time, the train was half empty. The two tall brothers, the twins, Nicholas and Alexander, were very similar in appearance while their younger brother was shorter and slighter, yet despite their differences, now they all had silver hair, you could see a strong family likeness.

When they weren't talking, they dozed off, having between them, very many years.

This, they had agreed, was their swan song. A last, joyful reunion, a few days in London, with their sister, now all of them together. It had been very special these days, and they were aware it would probably be the very last trip they would make.

"Come luxury Class, Alex," Algie had urged his elder brother. "Pull out the stops! Not only is it a special time for all of us, but it will be worth it, you will see." So Alex had crossed the Atlantic in a luxury liner, slightly apprehensive of this last, taxing journey, but all the same, with a quiver of excitement causing his dark eyes to twinkle. Algie hadn't said much, but the whole mystery sounded quite extraordinary and he was looking forward to meeting his younger brother's friends.

Nick merely had to fly from Paris, an easy hop, but even so, it was a long time since he had ventured from the security of his comfortable apartment overlooking the river.

They had both been beautifully looked after and felt so spoilt, so even considered coming again.

Their niece and nephew had met them at the airport and taken them to the old Karendski house, just South of London to be met by the youngest sibling, their sister Clarissa. There, the brothers rested and talked and talked, dozed off and talked again. The women anticipated their every need, so it seemed that time had stopped, for back in their old childhood home, they were all totally relaxed.

Now, well rested, they were on the train, travelling West. Algie told them something of his friends, but little of the exciting project which lay ahead. It was not every day that such an astonishing haul of old gem stones came to light, and it had been the perfect excuse to get them all together, probably for the last time. Algie was letting the secret out in dribs and drabs, determined that his brothers would enjoy the revelation ahead.

The taxi stood outside the station to meet them and the driver greeted Algie who he knew well by now. Luggage in, the brothers settled into their seats and gazed around. Despite a strong wind, it was a bright day and they drove through some beautiful country. The driver looked in his rear mirror and listened, wondering what language they were speaking. Funny thing, he had always thought that Mr. Algie was a true Brit, for his English was so perfect, but he seemed to be something else too. He would ask, and satisfy his curiosity later.

The twins were put up in the big house which they admired enormously. Built of soft grey stone, on a hill with distant views of the sea, it was surrounded by oaks, which their host told them were descendants of those great trees used in the past to build ships. England's glorious navy! When rested they were driven the short distance to Mrs. Eliot's house, a quaint little lodge by the gate. Here they had coffee and home made scones with cream and jam, and once again, relaxed and waited for the mystery to unfold. Coffee cups cleared, it seemed the time had come.

Roger Muir, who Algie had met so many years ago, when he was a young man in the army in India, and when Roger was a child, brought out an old, red leather case. They noted that Roger was probably Indian, very pale brown with grey/blue eyes. He seemed extremely civilized and relaxed, and Algie explained that he had grown up here, in the big house, so while being Indian by birth, he was in fact a West country Englishman.

Carefully, he lifted ancient papers, and laid them aside, till finally, he drew forth a sheath of drawings, beautifully executed, and spread them on the coffee table. Not a word was spoken while the two brothers carefully looked at the delicate drawings, then, observed the squat little carved work box sitting on the carpet. When, the drawings were back in their case, they proceeded, eyes bright with anticipation.

Next, Mrs. Eliot, who asked them to call her, "Madeline" put a glass bowl on the table, a bowl covered with a fine lace handkerchief, which she removed.

It was as if it were full of ice, for the contents were clear and sparkling with rainbow colours the sun shining through them. She put her fingers in and twirled the points of light about before pushing the bowl to her guests.

The twin Kardenski's reached out, and each with a pocket lens, examined first one, then another of the stones, nodding to each other.

"I just happened to choose the leg which held the diamonds," she said. "I suggest you three each choose your corner, and let's see who has what. Then, it will be up to you to sort out who wants whatever!" She laughed lightly and they all smiled at her.

Roger brought forth the workbox while she was speaking.

"Heavy little thing," he announced, carefully lowering it on to the coffee table on which Madeline had placed a thick cloth.

They watched silently as he removed the shelf, and once again, took up the two gold crochet hooks and fitted them into the slots to raise the false bottom of the base.

"I hope you won't mind if we offer Algie the first corner, as it has been he who has made all the arrangements, and who we entrusted with the whole project originally. Then, I think I will offer you two," she smiled at the twins, "the dice, so you can throw for who is next." They smiled and nodded their agreement.

It was indeed a strange sight, five elders grouped around an old, heavily carved workbox perched on the coffee table between them. This time, Roger used the electric iron to gently soften the beeswax and Algie chose his corner. Kitchen knife in hand, Roger gently chipped at the softened wax until it came up, revealing a dark cylindrical hole.

They took their time, Maddy and Roger, so that their guests could savour the moment.

Another glass bowl was brought out, and hooking about in the hole, Algie carefully drew out the twist of deep pink silk and let Madeleine snip the cord which held its secrets folded within. Holding the silk above the bowl they held their breaths as the sapphires tinkled into the bowl, a shimmer of blues cascaded with a sweet sound, then settled. They silently looked at it, impressed.

"Have a look, boys," said Algie, reaching into the bowl, his pocket lens poised to search into the depth of the stone he lifted out. "Karats upon karats, go on!"

There was silence as the three professionals took up a stone, and carefully gazed at it, then carefully put it to the side and chose another one and did the same.

Looking at each other, they smiled, nodding and murmured words of appreciation.

Laughing lightly, Madeline put a gaming cup with dice in it on the table.

"Highest score has next choice."

Alex picked up the cup, shook and cast the dice down, and his twin did like wise, but Alex had the higher score. "I was only fifteen minutes younger, anyway!" Nicholas announced to all their amusement.

So Alex's leg produced emeralds, while Nicholas' leg gave up its secret haul of rubies. Roger carefully removed the workbox, set it on its legs and then went back to the coffee table.

Four glass bowls stood together, glowing and sparkling with light and colour, their silk blankets of ages pushed to one side for the moment, but not to be discarded, for they were all part of the story. Unable to help themselves, the brothers kept on picking up stones, to peer into their depths, fascinated, impressed.

Alex took over, always the leader, if only the elder by fifteen minutes,

"Due to our different countries and cultures," he began, folding up his lens and tucking it into a breast pocket, "we know what stones are most sought after. As, thank goodness, we have always been an entirely united and cooperative family, we will have to work out who takes what. But," he turned his handsome face to Madeline, "as these belong to you, I do suggest that you take what you want for your own family now, before we swoop on them."

Maddy turned to Roger eyes enquiringly.

"What do you think, dearest? Something for each of the older children to pass on, a gift through me, from your grandmother?" He nodded,

"Lovely idea, but be sure they are yours, as she meant them to be. But I do think that you should choose, perhaps four, one of each and ask Karendskis to make up four rings, for the girls and wives. And something very special for you Madeline, unusual, superb, a proper memory of this strange event." They all nodded, murmuring their agreement, while Maddy and Roger smiled warmly at each other.

Then Alex spoke.

"For myself, I can see we have here a magnificent collection of cut and natural stones, many karats of them. But, imagine the interest, without any names mentioned, of course, of your story, the provenance? I know many people who will be as fascinated by it as are we. So, Roger, if you can write, or better, type it ALL out for us, this will certainly add to the value. Please make photo copies of the drawings, and each should take the silk wrapping, perhaps to put, for show, in a small glass case. Oh what fun, my friends, brothers, a real project, thank you from us all for involving us and allowing us to be the first to see them. As for payment, we will have to be advised by our sons, the gemmologists and cutters, and rest assured, you will receive, in time, the absolutely correct payment."

"Thank you for your words," Maddy felt a surge of affection for all of them. "We have already picked one, apart from the four we will choose later with your help, and perhaps Algie will choose some to make me an extraordinary ring, or brooch using four different stones." She went to the little side board, brought down an egg cup and took out a twist of kitchen paper. "We think it is a blue diamond, even if it looks like a sea pebble, so strange, of them all, just the one.

Roge says he remembers his grandmother always wearing it. Algie says it is most exciting."

The two brothers both reached for it, laughed, then passed it, one to the other.

"So wise, Madeline, for this is very rare, very valuable, although coloured diamonds used not to be worth anything years ago, and as there appears to be just one, I think it right for you to keep it or we might squabble!" They laughed gently and the egg cup and treasure went back on to the dresser.

They sat long into the night, busy with pocket lenses, exchanging views, lifting stones to the light, exclaiming, admiring, until Maddy phoned her son to come and collect her guests as it was getting late.

Roger sat, two fingers raised, and typed out the whole story with Madeline helping him, putting in a word here or there. Of course they did not know where the blue diamond had come from originally. Ayah, that poor and loving nursemaid, who had been given it by the rani's mother. Then in turn, she had given it to her much loved charge the rani, but that Roger's grandmother had it all her life, he did remember. They made the photo copies of the drawings at the big house, several copies and a couple for themselves.

He wrote about Maddy's father, without giving names, the unrequited love his grandmother had for him. Her inspiration to hold him for a little longer by building a hospital, still to this day, functioning, important in their small town. His own life in Britain, his return to India, then years and years later, Maddy visiting him and meeting the very old secretary, Filipe Mendoza, whose name he did mention, who had aided his grandmother so carefully and held her papers for her till the day before he died.

It went on and on, two full pages, how at first, merely puzzled, then really mystified, he had gone through the red leather box, the papers, then finding the sheets on astrology, old, fragile, amazing.

Finally then, back in England where Maddy had kept safely, her precious workbox, how together they opened it, and found the dowry the rani had collected together for the heaven meant bride for her beloved grandson.

Yes indeed, it would give interest to the people who bought the pieces which would eventually be made up, and sold in America, Britain and France.

Satisfied with their evening's work, the two loving souls went to bed, gently locked in each other's arms.

EPILOGUE

Christmas is over, and it was a good one. Uncle Algie came of course. Although he is very frail now and hardly ever goes out, as he lives just a few steps away, the boys escorted him here and I went back with him to help him to bed.

I feel so excited, like a young girl, and keep on looking at my hand where sits the wonderful present he gave me. It is a solitaire diamond ring, but with a difference. The diamond is an amazing and beautiful blue!

While I was in the kitchen putting the finishing touches to the lunch, he pottered in, apparently intent on getting me alone.

"Clare! My dear neice." He was fumbling about in his pocket. "I want to give you something very special to thank you for all your loving care of me over the years." A familiar green Karrendski box appeared, a ring box. He held it out towards me.

Quickly drying my hands I took it. Although my heart was beating fast, I didn't open it, wanting to savour the moment for both of us.

"It was a gift to me," he went on, "a stick pin in fact, which I wore but once, for a special occasion. It is, my child, very rare and very valuable, and I want you to have it before I die. Do not hesitate to wear it every day of your life, for it is safer on your hand than anywhere else." He waved his hand at the box impatiently, his eyes bright with anticipation. "Go on then, open it!"

Very, very slowly I did, peeping in as the lid lifted, and there, nestled in the white satin lay a ring set with a beautiful blue stone surrounded by tiny white diamonds. I looked up at him startled.

"No, my dear," he had his smug voice on, "it is not a sapphire, it is a diamond, a blue diamond. It didn't look like that when it was given to me, it seemed just a blue pebble. So I had it cut in Antwerp, and oh my, it is a wondrous stone and I am so very proud to hand it over to you." Impatient again he urged me, "Go on then, put it on, let us feast for Christmas and feast our eyes on perhaps the most beautiful blue diamond I have ever seen during my long years with gems."

I took it out of the box and slid it onto my finger beside my wedding band. It fitted perfectly, so I guessed that brother Tim had been involved. Suddenly feeling tearful and foolish, I feared I might weep. So instead I wrapped myself around Uncle Algie in an extravagant hug, kissed him hard and sniffed into his rough, tweed shoulder.

"Oh Uncle Algie, what a fantastic present! You have certainly made my Christmas. I shall treasure it always. Thank you, oh thank you." I felt very weepy.

He continued looking smug, a small smile on his face. "And I have noted that it matches the Knowledge blue eyes perfectly."

We laughed together, for I do believe he was right, even if his eyes have faded with age. We did inherit Clara's eyes, he and I, and happily my daughter Clarissa has them too. I lifted up my arm and whirled around the kitchen, hand up, in order to admire the precious jewel. Truly it was magnificent.

"Now Uncle, tell me, where on earth did you find it?" Foolish me to ask, for he clammed up, his mouth setting in the mulish look I knew so well. Due no doubt to his years of discretion working with jewels, gems and people, he is a secretive old boy.

"Don't ask me, Clare my child. I cannot tell you. But you are not without intelligence. You of all people know of my activities. Where I go, or should I say, went, as I go nowhere any more, and the company I keep. So I leave it to you to exercise some guesswork. You will reach the solution yourself in good time. But I have the written history of it for you, for after I'm dead. You will see it is a fascinating story of great love over many years. Meanwhile, enjoy your ring, do insure it well, never take it off, wear it every day." He stopped, smiling very happily at me, twinkling. "Now, what did I come over for? Oh yes! How about lunch?"

Printed in Great Britain
by Amazon.co.uk, Ltd.,
Marston Gate.